DAKOTA DEATH-TRAP

The Texas Trouble-Shooters had a mission; find and bring to justice the homicidal outlaws led by the notorious Blanco Duval. From Wyoming to the Dakotas, they stalked their quarry, and as always Danger was their companion. At the end, only the fastest guns could survive.

MARSHALL GROVER

---◆---

DAKOTA DEATH-TRAP

A Larry & Stretch Western

Complete and Unabridged

LINFORD
Leicester

First published in Australia by
Horwitz Grahame Pty Limited
Sydney

First Linford Edition
published January 1993
by arrangement with
Horwitz Grahame Pty Limited
Sydney

British Library CIP Data

Grover, Marshall
    Larry & Stretch: Dakota death-trap.
    —Large print ed.—
    Linford western library
    I. Title II. Series
    823 [F]

    ISBN 0–7089–7358–2

Published by
F. A. Thorpe (Publishing) Ltd.
Anstey, Leicestershire

Set by Words & Graphics Ltd.
Anstey, Leicestershire
Printed and bound in Great Britain by
T. J. Press (Padstow) Ltd., Padstow, Cornwall

1

The Bandit-Haters

HIS appearance encouraged respect, the stranger riding into Varney, South Wyoming. He was distinguished-looking, his riding clothes of expensive quality, and his mount was a handsome thoroughbred chestnut.

He rode two blocks of the main stem to reach Nader's Saloon and, as he dismounted and looped his rein, noted the damaged facade. A front window had been boarded up pending the arrival of replacement glass. Entering, he observed there was nothing left of the back bar mirror except its frame. The staircase had been repaired; timber used to reconstruct the balustrade had that new look.

At the bar, he asked for the proprietor.

1

"He know you?" asked the barkeep.

"I've never been here before. My name is Dexter Beech."

"Well, his name's Al Nader," offered the barkeep.

He sent a percentage-girl up to the saloonkeeper's office. The girl returned and, a few moments later, a lank-haired, sharply-tailored Al Nader appeared atop the stairs, frowning down at the newcomer.

"You want to see me?" he prodded.

"To discuss a little business," said Beech. "It will be to your advantage."

"All right, come on up," invited Nader.

Beech climbed the stairs and was conducted into Nader's office. He sat with the desk separating him from Nader and got right down to business.

"I heard about your trouble, the brawl here, the arrest of those notorious Texans."

"Bad news travels fast," grouched Nader.

"And far," said Beech. "My informant

was Hobie Tyne."

"Oh, sure, the peddler," nodded Nader. "He sure gets around."

"Always stops by when he's in our area," said Beech. "My ranch, Diamond B, is quite a trace north. And, as you know, Tyne's a great talker."

"Yeah, a real blabbermouth," agreed Nader. "So?"

"So I think we can do business," said Beech. "How much damage, Nader? And cost of repairs? Give me a rough figure."

"Hundred and twenty dollars," scowled Nader. "If they'd agreed to pay for the damage, I wouldn't've had the marshal lock 'em up. They could sure afford to. I know for a fact they deposited fourteen hundred in the Varney Trust Bank the morning they got here."

"I have work for Valentine and Emerson," declared Beech. "Does this sound fair enough to you? I hand you a hundred and twenty right now."

He produced his wallet. "You come to the town jail with me, withdraw your complaint, and I take them out of Varney."

Nader didn't hesitate; Beech would have been surprised if he had. $120 changed hands and, minutes later, they were walking downtown, Beech leading his chestnut.

Meanwhile, in adjoining cells of the poky town jail, the tough drifters relaxed. To be cooped up this way was no new experience for Lawrence Valentine and Woodville 'Stretch' Emerson. Being Lone Star stubborn, they preferred a thirty day hitch behind bars to parting with one dime of their joint bankroll. Hand $120 to the likes of Al Nader? *That'd* be the day. The brawl had been forced on them, as Nader was well aware, local roughnecks goading them by insulting their homestate, Nader unwisely assuming the ruckus would be short-lived. Well, the Texans' assailants had numbered five but, when the battle was over and the bar-room a shambles, their assailants were down and groaning and they still upright and showing minimal facial damage.

"We've had to eat worse chow," Larry remarked.

He squatted on the edge of his bunk, brawny, dark-haired and heavy-jawed, six feet three inches of case-hardened Texan. With his partner of nineteen years or more, he had outfought countless town rowdies, also desperadoes of every kind, rustlers, road agents, bank robbers, swindlers, cardsharps, homicidal gunslingers — every kind. And he was still a survivor, often disillusioned and cynical, but somehow retaining his sense of humor.

"The bunks're hard, but we've slept on harder," drawled Stretch. "Anyway, five more days and we're out of here. We collect our dinero from the bank and make tracks, so we should care?"

The taller trouble-shooter was horizontal on his bunk, which was too short for him. Well, naturally, his being a six-and-a-half-footer. Of more easy-going disposition than Larry, he was sandy-haired and lantern-jawed with jughandle ears, downright homely in fact.

So here they were, a couple of living legends with more cash than they could use for their routine needs, resenting their reputation and those they blamed for the building and wide circulation of that reputation, specifically the editors of frontier newspapers and the photographers who had recorded their weather-beaten faces for posterity. They referred to the freak circumstances that, on a regular basis, prodded them into life or death battles with the lawless, as their hex. Being somewhat single-minded, it rarely occured to them that they, not the Fourth Estate, had built the reputation; they were victims of their own altruism, knights errant to the core, and too old to change their ways.

Referring to Cyrus Creedy, Varney's town marshal, Larry glanced along the passage and muttered, "Sounds like that no-account badge-toter's got company. I hear a lot of talk."

"One of 'em's Nader, the dude that owns the saloon," said Stretch, cocking an ear. "Still bellyachin' I bet. Well, his place looked some toilworn by the time we got through mixin' it with them plug-uglies."

"Ain't that the truth," Larry agreed with relish.

The jailhouse door was unlocked. Pot-bellied Creedy came along the passage followed by the well-dressed stranger, squinted in at the prisoners and announced, "This gent's bailin' you out. Wants to parley with you, and then I'll be turnin' you loose." He nodded to Beech. "Take your time. When you're ready, just come rap on the door."

He returned to his office, closing the entrance door behind him. Left alone with the Texans, Beech ran his sad eyes over them and fished out cigars, Havanas. They rose and moved to the bars, accepted the cigars and a light. He lit his own from the same match.

"Not superstitious, are you?" he asked. They shook their heads, smoked and looked him over. "Buying you out of here is only part of what I'm willing to pay for your services. You can name your own price. I know you, Valentine, by reputation, you too, Emerson, and I believe you'll succeed where the law has failed. Wouldn't be the first time for you, right?"

"We've nailed a bandido or two in our time," shrugged Stretch, who tended to understate.

"How much did it cost you — Nader's damages?" asked Larry.

"Hundred and twenty," said Beech. "I can afford that much and a whole lot more."

"We're cosy enough here," Larry pointed out. "What we stashed in the local bank don't make us as rich as you, but it's a fortune to the likes of us."

"I'd add two thousand to it, more if

you want," declared Beech.

"You sound kind of desperate," frowned Larry.

"Unless the murdering outlaw known as Blanco Jack Duval is brought to justice, others will suffer as I have suffered." Pain showed in the rancher's eyes. Larry's sympathy was aroused and Stretch ill at ease; any show of emotion affected him this way. "The law keeps letting him slip through their fingers and I've little confidence in the Pinkertons, but plenty in you two. I respect your record. Look, will you at least accompany me to my spread up north? It would be the ideal place for you to begin your quest and, along the way, we could talk."

"Tell us here and now," urged Larry, "just how much has this Duval hombre cost you?"

Beech bowed his head.

"The three people nearest and dearest to me — and a lot of sleepless nights," he said softly.

Stretch winced and glanced at his

partner. He guessed the decision was made, and his guess was accurate; the expression on Larry's face was eloquent."

"Well," he said. "We got nothin' better to do."

"We'll load provisions, at my expense of course," said Beech. "The sooner we get started the better."

The trouble-shooters were shabby and hadn't bothered to shave since the morning before last but, to Beech, they appeared plenty formidable; he believed all he had heard and read of them.

"Sure," nodded Larry. "We only have to draw out our dinero, saddle up and sling our gear."

Beech retreated to the jailhouse door and knocked. Creedy came in again to unlock the Texan's cells. In his office, they retrieved their personal effects. Beech asked, as they strapped on their sidearms, "Will it take long for you to check out of your hotel?"

"Few minutes," shrugged Stretch.

The rancher was reminded the taller

Texan was ambidextrous with handguns. Their Colts were housed in tied-down holsters. Larry thonged down one holster, Stretch two; he packed a brace of .45s in holsters fixed to a buscadero-style shellbelt.

When they moved into the street, he asked while untying his chestnut, "Which stable?" Larry pointed. "All right, I'll pick up the provisions and wait for you there."

The tall men ambled to the bank to withdraw the bulk of their joint bankroll. It was stowed in Larry's hip-pocket, but only because his partner owned no wallet. They settled their bill at the hotel and collected their gear, then toted it to the stable and readied Larry's sorrel and Stretch's pinto. Their armory was impressive. As well as their sidearms, sheathed Winchesters were fixed to the horses along with packrolls and saddlebags.

They rode north out of Varney, flanking Beech, from whose saddle a sack of provisions dangled. At first, he held forth on a subject familiar to two tumbleweeds born and raised in the Texas Panhandle, the hardships of establishing a big cattle spread, the bad winters, the protection of breed-stock against rustler gangs and marauding redskins.

Night-camped on the north bank of the Sweet-water after an easy fording, they squatted about their cookfire and caught up on talk. The trouble-shooters knew little about the bandit gang led by Blanco Jack Duval; Beech knew plenty.

"Duval's the only one on record," he told them. "He was in custody about a year ago. A Dakota sheriff held him long enough for him to be photographed, but not to stand trial. His men raided the jail and broke him out. They go masked, so only Duval's been identified. I can show you one of the handbills when we reach Diamond B. Believe me, you'll know him when you find him — as I'm sure you will, no matter how long it takes."

"Kind of special is he?" asked Stretch.

"Clean-shaven . . . " The rancher listed details bitterly, as though every word left a bad taste in his mouth. "Pale blue eyes and pink complexion. Height about six feet, strongly-built. And the nickname fits." He gestured to the taller Texan. "You're fair-haired. Some would call you blond. Duval's hair is even lighter, almost white."

Larry downed a well-masticated mouthful and surmised, "The gang's got a hideout no posse could find."

"Rumored to be somewhere in the Black Hills," nodded Beech.

"They've robbed banks and stage-coaches all over Dakota, Wyoming and Colorado, Nebraska too."

"Always a clean getaway," mused Stretch.

"Sometimes pursuit parties get too close, only to ride into an ambush," said Beech. "They're trigger-happy and, when it comes to shooting their way out of a township, they're not particular about their targets. Many an unarmed bystander has been cut down." When he was through eating, he filled his cup from the coffeepot and remarked, "Money doesn't seem important to you, but you might as well know the price on Duval's head now stands at five thousand dollars."

"That'd be important if we were bounty hunters, but we ain't," said Stretch.

Talking, or maybe the journey south from his ranch, must have tired Beech. Before rolling into his blanket, he thought to explain how he had ascertained their whereabouts; the visit to Diamond B of the gabby peddler.

"Hobie Tyne's always welcome. Of all the Pegrum County spreads, mine is farthest from the county seat, so Tyne can usually count on making a sale or two."

His companions had to control their curiosity. They travelled north two more days before he again referred to sleepless nights and the three people nearest and dearest to him. At a fork of the trail, he gestured to a signpost. The township of Pegrum lay three miles north. To reach Diamond B, they would take the right fork, making northeast. They rode on after spelling the horses, and it was now that he confided, "When able to visit town, I go first to the cemetery."

"Nearest and dearest, you said back in Varney," Larry recalled. "Brother and sister?"

Beech shook his head dolefully.

"My wife — my two sons."

"Sorry," frowned Larry.

"Ritchie and Hollis weren't yet of age," signed Beech.

"Just sixteen and eighteen. Good boys. From the time they were old enough to sit a horse, they insisted on taking their turn at working the herd, hunting strays, joining the trail drives."

He muttered a curse. "Duval and his nine killers will steal anything. They favor banks and stagecoaches, but are just as likely to hit the cattlemen."

"They tried to rustle Diamond B stock?" prodded Stretch.

"In broad daylight," Beech said softly. "Our southeast quarter, the most remote section of Diamond B range. Ritchie and Hollis were flushing strays there when the raiders showed up — shooting. Young Ritchie wasn't given time to draw. He must've been killed instantly. The sound of gunfire brought other hands to the scene, so the raiders cut and ran, escaped to the east. My foreman found Ritchie dead with his pistol still holstered. Hollis didn't die rightaway. His gun was in his hand, only one bullet fired. He survived just long enough to identify Duval. He'd studied the handbill you see, and the local paper, the *Courier*, had reported one of the stage holdups and run Duval's picture. Of course Sheriff Riordan had no chance of heading them off this side of the border."

Larry nodded soberly and commented,

"You sure got a right to crave Duval's head."

"Two funerals," said Beech, grimacing. "Then, three weeks later, a third. Madeline, my wife, the shock and grief were just too much for her. She suffered a heart attack. A doctor was brought to the ranch as quickly as possible, but there was nothing he could do for her." He darted glances right and left at the tall men flanking him. "And Blanco Jack still rides free — damn him!"

"Just till we run him to ground, Mister Beech," muttered Larry.

"Yup," grunted Stretch. "Just till then."

"So you'll do it — go after him?" Beech asked eagerly.

"We'll do it," nodded Larry.

Beech heaved a sigh and thanked them fervently, also adding a warning.

"Better if you leave from the ranch. The chuck-boss will see you have ample provisions. You should stay far clear of Pegrum. There'd be nothing but

17

trouble for you there, the kind you don't appreciate."

"Why so?" frowned Stretch.

"Roy Riordan, the county sheriff, hates all Texans and is jealous of your reputation," said Beech. "That goes for his deputies too and most of the townsfolk. A lot of ill-feeling toward southerners in the country seat."

"Yeah, well, you're right," said Stretch. "We don't crave that kind of aggravation."

"It's been five months since I buried my sons and their mother," Beech said sombrely. "Five months of waiting and hoping to read of Duval's death or capture. Then when the peddler told us of the incident at Varney and you two stuck in the town jail, I felt hope for the first time since losing my wife and sons. If anybody can flush those killers out . . ."

"No guarantees," cautioned Larry. "We get lucky . . ."

"More often than not," interjected Stretch.

"But we're only human," Larry pointed out. "So no promises, no guarantees. We'll just give it our best shot."

"I couldn't hope for more," declared Beech. "But, for your own sake, remember this. Trying to take Duval alive could be the death of you. I've read all the reports, so I know his style. He's the kind who, when the chips are down would *pretend* to surrender — you follow me?"

"Way ahead of you," said Larry. "If he unbuckled his iron, there'd be a hideaway gun in a pocket or inside of his hat."

"It'll be kill or be killed, make no mistake about that," insisted Beech.

"We'll keep that in mind," Stretch assured him.

"It was 4 p.m. when, after skirting the Diamond B herd, the riders came into view of the ranch headquarters. The Texans were impressed. Handsome was the word for the big two-storeyed ranch-house, and every other building was sound, no ramshackle structures here, no corrals in need of repair, the barn and bunkhouse of solid construction; they could believe Diamond B was the biggest and most prosperous spread in Pegrum County.

After they rode into the area fronting the house, Beech was welcomed home by his foreman, the lean, jovial Nick Tresler.

"Good to see you again, Dex. And, by golly, you found 'em and fetched 'em." He offered his hand as the Texans dismounted. "Larry Valentine and Stretch Emerson, I call this an honor."

Beech performed introductions. Two others came to the fore, hefty waddies aiming genial nods at the trouble-shooters.

"Ames and Cuttle," offered Beech. "Two of my most trusted hands. They'll take care of your horses. Nick, our guests will dine with me this evening and head east after an early breakfast." He eyed the Texans enquiringly. "Does that suit you?"

"Suits us fine," decided Larry.

"You'll sleep in comfort tonight," Beech predicted.

"Good bunkhouse," guessed Stretch.

"Not for you the bunkhouse," said Beech. "I'll have one of the servants air the bedroom Ritchie and Hollis used to share."

The tall men washed up before supper, but did not shave. Stretch wanted to know why. Larry promised to explain after their departure. The meal was to their liking and, during it, their host showed them the reward dodger on their quarry and a recent edition of the county newspaper.

"The gang's last strike," he told them. "I don't know if you'll pick up a lead in Maddenville, a town just beyond the border in Dakota, but I'm guessing that's where you'll start from. They robbed the First National Bank there a short time back."

"Maddenville'll do for starters," decided Larry. "Headed east for

Dakota, will we find another town?"

"I think so," said Beech. "Don't remember its name, but yes, there's at least a settlement this side of the border. You're anticipating re-provisioning there?"

"Might have to," said Larry. "Depends on what fresh meat we can shoot 'fore we get there."

While downing a refill of coffee, Stretch scanned the newspaper story and gave vent to his disgust.

"Says here they left the bank manager with a slug in his shoulder and a cashier dead — gun-whipped the poor sonofagun. And the Maddenville badge-toters couldn't get a clear bead on 'em when they made their break."

"Used the other cashier and a couple of women as shields," nodded Larry. "The Duval bunch — and many another wolf pack we've hunted."

They turned in early and slept deeply that night. Ten minutes after sunrise, they were up and bathed and dressed, ready to account for a hearty breakfast and make for the east trail. As assured by Beech, the chuck-boss had packed an ample supply of provisions into a couple of sacks. They secured these when they were saddled up with all gear slung and ready to mount.

The farewell was warm. Last to shake their hands, Beech earnestly urged them, "Remember everything I've told you of Duval. Take no chances. Stop him once and for all, but don't let the Duval gang be the last owlhoot gang you'll account for."

"We'll be rememberin' your wife too," muttered Larry. "And your boys."

"Yes." The rancher nodded wistfully. "Keep them in mind — always."

"There'll be one hulluva celebration when you get back," enthused Tresler.

"Not for the beanpole and me," Larry said as they swung astride. "Won't be no need for us to head back here. Everything you want to know, you'll read it in the newspapers anyway."

"Part of the legend, Nick," said

Beech. "They're rarely seen again in a place they've visited." He raised a hand. The tall riders were wheeling their mounts, pointing them eastward. "Safe travelling, boys. Get the job done, but not at the cost of your lives."

"Some of the hands hanging around the bunkhouse called encouragement, watching the Texans ride out. Again, they guided their horses around or through bunched Diamond B steers, sleek animals, hides gleaming in the morning sunlight. No conversation till Beech's lush acres were far to their rear and they were following the ramrod's directions to join the stage trail leading to South Dakota.

"Saddest hombre we've run into in a good long time, Dex Beech," Stretch commented.

"He'll likely never smile again till he finds out Duval can't do no more killin'," mused Larry. "Sure, he's a sad one, and he's got cause."

Easy-going Stretch rarely gave voice

to profound statements but, like his partner, he kept thinking of Beech's personal losses.

"I guess we're fortunate we stayed bachelor, never took wives nor sired kids," he muttered. "I don't know how I'd feel if it happened to me, two sons gunned down by bandidos, their momma dyin' of grief. Chances are I'd go plumb loco."

"The less we got to lose, the less we got to mourn," Larry said pensively.

Abruptly, Stretch reverted to another subject.

"We still own razors," he said pointedly.

"Better we forget our razors, maybe till we're through with this chore," said Larry.

"If you say so," shrugged Stretch. "But tell me why."

"You and me, we're a whole lot like some of the scum we've had to fight — in one way," reasoned Larry. "Our pictures've been in too many damn newspapers. Too many hard cases know too much about us, which makes it too easy for 'em to peg us anyplace we show ourselves."

"Keep on talkin'," urged Stretch, squinting. "I'm listenin' careful and trying' to savvy."

"We just never change," Larry went on. "We're stuck in our ways."

"No argument," shrugged Stretch.

"A pinto's your favorite mount," said Larry. "Me, I like a sorrel. It's like a habit. You pack two Colts because you're as gun-smart left-handed as with your right. We're too easy to recognize."

"I'm startin' to catch your drift," frowned Stretch.

"This time out, we ought to make some changes," said Larry.

"What kind of changes?" demanded Stretch. "And don't forget there's some things we *can't* change. We can't talk any other way — we don't know how — and we're still as tall. No way we could suddenly get shorter."

"Sure, but we can do *somethin'*,

damn it," insisted Larry. "Got plenty wampum, right? So we can buy different clothes in the next town we find. We can let our whiskers grow. And we can buy different horses, maybe a black for you and a white for me." Hell, we could even change our names."

"I'll be dogged." Stretch was taken aback.

"Am I talkin' crazy?" challenged Larry. "Is this a dumb notion?"

Stretch did some thinking and conceded, "Maybe not. And quittin' shavin' sure beats usin' fake beards. Where the hell'd we find fake whiskers anyway?"

The rain began an hour after their brief noon-camp and, when they came to a crossroads, they were shrouded in their slickers with their Stetsons dripping. The signpost told them the settlement of Bullivant's Bend was some twenty miles due south and that the next town east, Castleton, was closer; they could make it before nightfall.

"Castleton," Larry said as they pushed on east. "That'll be the town Beech spoke of, last town before we make Maddenville on the border." After another mile of riding the rain-swept trail, he asked, "how d'you feel about a new shellbelt?"

"Howzat again?" prodded Stretch.

"With only one holster," said Larry. "Seems every hard case and tin star knows Emerson travels double gunhung."

"Well, yeah, maybe," said Stretch. "I guess I could keep my other iron in my saddlebag — till I need it." He winced and shook his head. "Hell, runt. We won't just *look* different. We'll *feel* different."

"It's just an idea, worth tryin'," opined Larry.

3.45 that afternoon, when they ambled their mounts into the west end of Castleton's main street, that muddy thoroughfare and its plank sidewalks were deserted, for the obvious reason; who'd want to be out and about in such heavy rain? But Larry wasn't about to complain. This way, their arrival would be unnoticed.

Their first impulse was to head for a saloon, but they changed their minds when, in the second block along, they sighted an establishment proclaimed by its fresh-painted shingle to be the premises of Tex Harrick — Gents' Apparel. Stretch grinned as they pointed the horses toward the clothing store.

"Got to be one of our kind, runt. What hombre'd have the nerve to call himself Tex if he was Montana-born?"

"If he ain't Texan, he's gonna be plumb ashamed," predicted Larry.

The alley west of the store was narrow enough to provide temporary shelter for the sorrel and pinto. They swung down and, on the sidewalk in front of the closed door, removed their wet slickers and shook water off their Stetsons.

The door jingled a bell as they

29

opened it and entered. Stretch re-closed it and, from the rear, the proprietor appeared. It had been said they bred 'em tall in Texas, but this broad-grinning man was an exception, standing no higher than five-feet-seven, portly and balding.

"By damn!" he exclaimed. "Larry Valentine and . . . ! He dropped his voice when Larry raised a finger to his lips, "and Stretch Emerson, as I live and breathe."

His mode of speech, the familiar accent, proved his nickname was no affectation. Given name Warren, he told them, but always known as Tex. Was he delighted to meet them? An understatement. He shook their hands and declared this a proud moment for him; he had followed their career with keen interest. "We're a long way from the old Lone Star, Tex," Larry remarked as they hung their dripping slickers on pegs near the street-door. "You know we can't shake our wander-itch, but what's your excuse?"

"Holy matrimony," explained Tex. "Cassie, the wife, has a lot of kin in and around Castleton. Wouldn't be fair, taking her all the way back to Texas. Damn fine woman. Deserves the best. I learned the tailoring trade from my pa back in Forth Worth, started this store fifteen years ago and we've been doing pretty good ever since. Well now, this sure is a pleasure, and what can I do for you fiddlefoots?"

"First thing, and it's mighty important, forget who we are," begged Larry. "There's this chore we got to take care of and it might give us an edge if we don't look like who we are . . ."

"Change our names for a while," offered Stretch. "Get rigged in different duds, and stuff like that."

"Hey now . . . !" breathed Tex, his eyes gleaming.

"Hey now what?" Larry asked warily.

"Where do you go from here?" demanded Tex.

"Dakota," said Larry.

"I should've guessed!" Tex snapped

his fingers. "Blanco Duval! You're outlaw-hunting again! Why do I say again? Hell, you're at it all the time." He hastened to assure them, "I won't shoot off my mouth, not even to Cassie. If anybody learns you're after the Duval bunch, they won't learn it from me."

"He's a fast guesser," Stretch remarked to Larry.

"That's no problem," decided Larry. "We can count on Tex."

"Gonna disguise yourselves, huh?" prodded Tex.

"Different duds," nodded Stretch. "Runt, what kind? You want us to look like farmhands, prospectors, what?"

"Sportin' gents maybe," frowned Larry. "Plenty pro gamblers around. They show up everywhere."

"Pants to be lengthened, sleeves too." Tex now ran a professional eye over them. "Yeah, I can fix you up. Got some tall size rig in stock but, when I say tall, I don't mean long-legged enough for you boys. Could have 'em ready for you tomorrow morning. That okay?"

"We'll be obliged," Larry thanked him. "And listen, amigo, we ain't busted. We're good for whatever it costs."

"Sure," grinned Tex. "But I cut my price just the same. For a fellow-Texan, always a special price."

"Could you store the clothes we're wearin'?" asked Larry.

"Any stuff you leave with me, it'll be laundered and waiting for you when you come back to Castleton," Tex assured him. "Now how about horses? Those cayuses of yours could be a dead giveaway."

"We already thought of that," said Stretch. "We'll be switchin' horses too."

"So here's what you do," offered Tex. "The Double A Livery and Barn along the street a little ways. Cassie's brother runs it. You ask for Alonzo Ackerby — he's called Lonz — tell him I sent you and I guarantee he'll be as close-mouthed as me and make you a good deal. Renting'd be best, and your animals'd get good care till you come back for 'em. Sounds okay?"

"Sounds fine," nodded Larry.

"You'll be overnighting here," Tex guessed. "Garvin Hotel's cheap and clean and the grub's passable."

He reached for a tape, took and wrote down some measurements and sent them on their way. They collected their horses and, a few minutes later, were talking turkey with Tex Harrick's brother-in-law.

2

Hesky Rhymes With Pesky

SCRAWNY, beak-nosed Lonz Ackerby gave the tall men his full attention while they offsaddled their animals and bedded them in stalls. He was prepared to be as discreet as Tex, and as co-operative; it was at his suggestion that they decided they must rent second-hand saddles as well as horses. Like his brother-in-law, Ackerby had an eye for detail.

"Double-cinched saddles're mostly favored by Texans," he pointed out. "You can't change the way you talk, but no sense advertising, huh? I'll show you some saddles and then you can choose horses. You don't have to buy. I'll rent 'em to you for as long as you need 'em."

Stretch was becoming optimistic

about his partner's change of identity ruse; the eager assistance of Tex Harrick and Lonz Ackerby was a boost to his spirits.

"I'm near gettin' to like the idea," he remarked while they inspected horses.

"Well, like Lonz said," Larry reminded him, "no sense advertisin'."

They decided on strong-limbed geldings, assured by Ackerby they were sound of wind and good for as much speed as would be required of them; Larry chose the dapple, Stretch the strawberry roan.

The rain was easing when they quit the barn, hefting their gear and making for the Garvin Hotel. They made a stop before reaching the hotel. Another store, this time a gunsmithery-cum-leathergoods store. There, the taller Texan purchased a shell-belt with holster attached right of its buckle.

They were drawing closer to the hotel and suddenly slowing their pace, remembering another necessary change.

"Names," Larry said pensively. "And we're gonna have to be careful when we reach Maddenville. By ourselves, where nobody else can hear, it don't matter. But . . . "

"But any place else, we better not forget our new monickers," muttered Stretch. "Careful? Hell, we got to be *mighty* careful."

"What d'you want to be called?" asked Larry.

"How in tarnation'd I know?" shrugged Stretch. "*You* think of a handle."

Never stuck for an alias, Larry decided then and there.

"All right, you're Brazos Billy Terhune and I'm Waco Webb."

"I guess I can remember that," said Stretch.

They moved on, toted packrolls, saddlebags and sheathed Winchesters into the hotel lobby and traded nods with the reception clerk. Larry paid for their overnight stay and scribbled W. J. Webb in the register. Stretch registered as W. E. Terhune while the clerk took a key from its hook.

"Number Three upstairs. Two soft beds guaranteed changed daily, no bugs. Dining-room opens six-fifteen for supper, same time for breakfast. Enjoy your stay, gents."

In Room 3 upstairs, while Larry straddled a chair and smoked, Stretch squatted on the edge of the bed of his choice and began rubbing dubbin inside his new holster.

"So what happens in Maddenville?" he wanted to know.

"We act like a couple driftin' sportin' men," said Larry.

"Ain't long since they had a bank robbery, so folks'll still be talkin' about it. We use our ears. Might be we'll pick up a lead without havin' to ask questions. If we do ask questions, we keep it casual. Just curiosity, okay? Couple strangers stop by a town like Maddenville, they're just naturally curious about what's been happenin' there."

"Guess so," agreed Stretch. "And, if we're supposed to be sportin' men, we better gamble some." "Right," nodded Larry. "You could hang around the roulette layout in whatever saloon we choose, maybe shoot dice too. I'll find a friendly poker party. 'Tween deals, poker players get to talkin'."

"You forgettin' the law?" frowned Stretch. "Damn near every town we visit, there's a sheriff or a town marshal got a file on us. And some badge-toters got long memories and sharp eyes. We can't hope to be in that town, even for a little while, and not get spotted by a tin star."

"That'll be a test," Larry realized, stroking his sprouting mustache, feeling at his stubbled jowls and chin. "The whiskers, the new duds and the horses — are they gonna fool a lawman? Well . . . " he shrugged fatalistically, "we'll find out, won't we?"

"If a badge-toter does spot us . . . " began Stretch.

"None of 'em hold warrants on us,"

said Larry. "If they want to know why we're usin' fake names and tryin' to look different, we can always tell 'em the truth."

"We scarce ever do *that*," Stretch protested.

"The kind of truth they'll believe," Larry assured him. "We've had our bellyful of hotheads recognizin' us on sight and proddin' us into a hassle, so we rigged a few changes."

"Sounds reasonable," mused Stretch. "But that'll kind of depend on how reasonable the badge-toters are."

"Like I said." Larry blew a smoke-ring. "We'll find out."

After supper, they strolled the main street a while, but gave the Castleton saloons a wide berth. They turned in early and, next morning, carried their gear down to the lobby and were first into the dining-room for breakfast.

Tex Harrick was ready for them when they entered his store.

"Stash your stuff," he urged. "Peel to your Long Johns behind that curtain and try these for size."

The cotton shirts and black serge pants were a comfortable fit, much to their gratitude. There were no early customers, so they had the store to themselves when they emerged from behind the curtain to inspect other items, celluloid collars, cravats of not too flashy pattern and checkered vests. When they had donned those items, Tex proffered coats, grey with a subdued stripe for Larry, black for Stretch. Tex assured them these were the best he could manage on such short notice, as they slipped them on.

"They'll do," Larry decided. "Not too tight around the shoulders. That's what matters. How about you, beanpole?"

"Comfortable enough," announced Stretch.

He strapped on his new gunbelt and thonged the holster down. Larry followed his example, after which Tex asked, "What kind of tiles?" The trouble-shooters winced.

"I know a lot of gamblers wear

41

derbies or high hats ... " began Larry.

"Aw, hell," groaned Stretch.

"A lot, but not all of 'em," reflected Larry.

"Sure," agreed Tex. "A sporting man's apt to wear any kind of hat. But — uh — those Stetsons of yours wouldn't match up with the new outfits. Tell me your head size. I'm suggesting black for you and grey for Stretch."

In a matter of moments, the tall men were inspecting themselves in a full-length mirror. Quite a change, they conceded. Nothing they could do to disguise their generous height, but the new outfits and short beards would help. Tex was proud of his efforts on their behalf. They selected spare shirts and Larry expressed their appreciation by adding $20 to their overall bill. Tex protested. Both trouble-shooters insisted, so he accepted the extra and earned their further appreciation by mentioning a detail they had overlooked.

"Cigars?" Larry was exasperated, but not with Tex. "*I* should've thought of that."

"The way you tearaways build a smoke of Bull Durham — onehanded — is typical cowhand," cautioned Tex. "Only once in a blue moon would a gambling man roll a cigarette that way. Most of 'em smoke cigars. Now and then you'll see a pipe-smoking tinhorn, but Long Nines're what they usually smoke. Havanas if they're high rollers and well-heeled."

"Thanks for rememberin', amigo," said Larry. "We'll buy some on our way to Lonz's place."

"Leave your old duds where you dropped 'em, I'll take care of 'em," said Tex, as they picked up their gear. "Take care now. Stay Lone Star lucky, huh?"

"You betcha," grinned Stretch.

"When I see you again, I'll want to hear all about how you licked the Duval gang," Tex insisted. "And, if you aren't in a big hurry, we could have us a few drinks and Cassie could fix us a fine supper."

"You got a deal, Tex, and thanks for everything," said Larry.

On their way to the stable, they did remember to stop by a store and buy cigars. The obliging Lonz Ackerby had the dapple and the strawberry roan saddled and ready for them. They thanked him as warmly as they had thanked his brother-in-law, attached packrolls, saddlebags and rifles and got mounted.

Out of Castleton they rode. Next stop Maddenville.

★ ★ ★

Life goes on, even in a town recently visited by trigger-happy bank bandits.

Mid-morning of the day before the Texans arrived, the citizens of Maddenville were caught up their regular chores. It was business as usual at, for instance, the tonsorial parlour run by barber Gus Torvill.

Well, almost. The customer in the swivel chair was Deputy Sheriff Luke Harroway and the man waiting his turn Floyd Cooney, a bartender at the Broken Arrow Saloon.

Harroway was irate and cursing lustily, his left ear bloody, Torvill dabbing at it with a shaving towel, trying to placate him and, at the same time, reprimanding his nephew and apprentice, the youngster responsible for the nick in the lawman's ear. Pudgy Torvill was scathing; a newcomer would immediately have realized this was not the first time young Enoch Hesky had incurred his uncle's displeasure.

"Told you a hundred times, you jackass. Point off the scissors to line out round the ear, but gently, never jabbing. Sorry about this, Deputy Harroway. I'll finish this job. Boy, you just stand by and watch, pay attention, hear?"

"Look what your ten-thumbed kid's done to my hair!" raged Harroway. "You got your gall, Gus Torvill, letting him practice on me!"

"I'll correct his mistakes," soothed the barber. "The only thing is it'll have to be a shorter haircut this time, but you'll look fine, just leave everything to me."

"Awful sorry, Mister Harroway," mumbled young Enoch.

"You're the peskiest pest in Maddenville — and damn useless," scowled the deputy.

"Listen, you dumb brat," growled Cooney. "You better quit hangin' round the saloon and tryin' to make time with the hired girls, else Tully Stedman'll have the bouncer throw you out."

Lawman and barkeep denounced the youth at some length. He stood grimacing, embarrassed, but also resigned; the indignation of his elders was no novelty to Enoch Hesky. At age sixteen, he was homely, thanks to buckteeth, a turned up nose and a thatch of brown hair that seemed to grow every which way. Physically, well, maybe he would fill out as he grew older, maybe add a few inches to his height. Right now, however, he was of slight build and just five feet five inches tall.

"Clumsy and good for nothing is what you are," declared Harroway. "Every job since you quit school, you've failed at."

"Hughie Cottrell kicked him out of his store when he'd been workin' there only two days," sneered Cooney. "Bad enough he irritated the hell out of Hughie's customers, he was all the time proposin' to Hughie's daughter and — hell's sakes — Imogene ain't sixteen yet!"

"He wasn't any more use the two weeks he worked for the carpenter," growled Harroway. "Couldn't even hammer a nail straight."

"Wasn't worth cold beans at the McCubbin ranch," recalled Cooney. "Couldn't learn to work cattle and, as a cook's helper, he almost got Jeb Whicker fired — spilled a mess of cayenne paper in the stew."

"You think me and the wife enjoy

having him around?" grouched Torvill, with scant regard for the youth's feelings. "We took him in after Dorrie's sister died and then her brother-in-law too, because that made him an orphan and we figured we had to do our Christian duty, but he's making nervous wrecks of us. The only thing he's good with is that Winchester he won. I bought him a horse so he could go hunting — hoping he'd get lost in the high country — but he always finds his way home."

"Uncle Gus, I've fetched home plenty jackrabbits," protested Enoch. "And, once a whole deer."

"That deer was ready to die of old age anyway," retorted Torvill, busy with scissors and comb. "Go on, sweep up the hair like I showed you."

Enoch began plying a broom over the hair-littered floor and, moments later, Floyd Cooney loosed a gasp and jerked upright.

"Awful sorry," frowned Enoch.

"What . . . ?" began Torvill.

"Consarn the brat!" yelled Cooney. "He near prodded my eye with the end of that damn broom!"

To the approval of his uncle and the deputy, Enoch was seized by Cooney and thrown out to the sidewalk. He fell face-down and passers-by showed no reaction, so accustomed were they to seeing him ejected from so many places, his uncle's barber shop, the Cottrell emporium, the saloons, even the local churches. He was, despite his eagerness to please, extremely unpopular, his clumsiness earning him a reputation as a disaster on two legs and a menace to the community.

It wasn't fair, he reflected, after picking himself up and meandering along Main Street. Why couldn't Uncle Gus and Aunt Dorrie be patient and try to understand him? Why couldn't the entire Maddenville population acknowledge that he was ambitious and striving to make a future for himself? Though only sixteen, he was already thinking as a grown man, or so he deluded himself.

Nearing the next corner, he stood aside respectfully, making way for a woman in black. First time he'd been this close to Mrs Cora Drummond, widow of the cashier slain during the bank holdup, close enough to address her; he decided he should do so.

"'Morning, Mrs. Drummond. I'm real sorry about Mister Drummond." She paused, distracted, eyeing him uncertainly. "Enoch Hesky, ma'am?"

"Oh, Enoch." She nodded. "Yes. Thank you." She stared along the street, barely aware of him now, and wondered aloud, "How many other women have been made widows by that outlaw — and how many more will there be?"

She continued on her way. He resumed ambling and, after crossing Main, came to the office fronting the Madden County Jail, the headquarters of the sheriff. There he paused for an intent scrutiny of the reward notice tacked to the front wall. In bold print above the picture of the notorious desperado, he read the enticing words: WANTED, DEAD OR ALIVE, $5000 REWARD.

He was still studying the poster when the heavyset, bushy-browed county sheriff appeared in the office doorway, eyeing him in grim amusement.

"What now?" challenged Francis P. O'Gorman. "You thinking of turning bounty hunter?"

The leg-pull drew a wistful response from Enoch.

"All that money, Sheriff, a whole five thousand dollars. I'd really have a future. Why, I could set myself up in business for instance."

"Sure, easy money," O'Gorman said poker-faced. "Nothing to it. All you have to do is find Duval's hideout, persuade him you aren't just a dumb kid, talk him into surrendering to you, then take him to the nearest law office. Mind now he mightn't agree to surrender at all, and his trigger-happy buddies'd likely shoot your butt off,

51

but that oughtn't bother a hot shot like you."

Enoch wandered on full of wild, reckless ideas. True, he made a hash of almost everything he attempted, but he did have one talent, just one. He was good with his Winchester, very accurate, rarely missing his target. Uncle Gus had paid for his black pony, but not the Winchester; he had won that fine weapon competing in the rifle shoot last 4th July, using a borrowed Sharps. With pistols he was useless, a menace in fact, but he could score with his Winchester nine times out of ten. Question: Could he work up the nerve to aim and shoot at a human target? He would have to think about that.

Deputy Harroway's minor but painful ear injury made it obvious Enoch could never become a safe barber. He doubted his uncle wished to continue tutoring him; if he had made a hash of cutting hair, it figured Uncle Gus wasn't about to risk his attempting to shave a customer. So, again, he needed employment.

Grudgingly, against his better judgement, livery stable-owner Carl Engle agreed to his helping out around the barn.

The Texans, reaching Maddenville early afternoon of the following day, decided to put their disguises to the acid test when, after ambling their mounts along only a block and a half of the main street, they sighted two defenders of the peace on the east sidewalk, Sheriff O'Gorman and the lean, sharp-featured Deputy Bob Lundine.

"What d'you say?" Larry asked softly.

"Might's well get it over and done with," shrugged Stretch. They veered their animals toward the lawmen, Larry raising a hand in friendly greeting. O'Gorman and Lundine paused to eye the new arrivals as they reined up.

"'Afternoon, gents," nodded Larry. "Glad we spotted you rightaway. For what we want to know, a lawman's the one to ask."

"All right, you're asking Frank O'Gorman, sheriff of Madden County," said O'Gorman, "and Deputy Sheriff Bob Lundine."

"Waco Webb," offered Larry. "My friend here, he's Brazos Billy Terhune."

"Howdy," drawled Stretch.

"And you got a question?" prodded Lundine.

"One you've been asked before, I guess," said Larry. "If you had to name a saloon where a sportin' man can find a little action, where the games're on the square, no sharpers, no loaded dice . . . ?"

"I come down heavy on every kind of cheater," the sheriff gruffly broke in. "We police the gambling houses all the time, so I'd say there's not much danger you'll get gypped." He glanced at his deputy. "Stedman's place?"

"Oh, sure," Lundine agreed. "No trick dealers at Stedman's. He'd never hire a crooked dealer." For the Texans' benefit, he gestured uptown. "The Broken Arrow, corner of Main and Grice."

"Much obliged," acknowledged Larry.

"Nice talkin' to you," nodded Stretch.

They resumed their northward progress along Main Street, quietly congratulating themselves.

"It worked," Larry said triumphantly.

"Yup, I'll swear they ain't onto us," muttered Stretch, glancing over his shoulder. "They ain't starin' after us, ain't lookin' leery."

"The whiskers, the new duds, the horses," grinned Larry.

"Question is, can we keep on foolin' 'em?" frowned Stretch.

"We mightn't have to stay long enough for 'em get curious," said Larry. "If we're gonna pick up any leads, it could happen tonight, so we'd be ridin' on manana."

Engle's Livery & Barn was sighted after they passed the First National Bank and the Broken Arrow. They dismounted out front and, as they led their horses into the stable, runty Carl Engle approached from the rear end, nodding a greeting.

"Got a couple stalls for our critters?" asked Stretch.

"Sure have," said Engle. "For how long?"

"Maybe just overnight," said Larry.

The livery-owner was less than four feet away when all three of them froze in shock. It hurtled between Engle and the Texans, its prongs embedding in the post separating two stalls, its haft quivering. Stretch's scalp crawled. The business end of the pitchfork had swished past his face with only inches to spare.

"Hol-eee Hannah!" he breathed.

"What in blue blazes . . . ?" gasped Engle. He whirled to stare up to the hayloft. "Hesky! You — you . . . !"

Enoch's head and shoulders appeared. He blinked worriedly and began an abject apology.

"Awful sorry, Mister Engle. It just

56

— slipped out of my hands. I — uh — must've lost my grip . . . "

"Come down out of there, damn you!" cried Engle. "Don't use the ladder, just jump! This could be Maddenville's lucky day! You might break your no-good neck!"

"Close," sighed Larry, a rivulet of sweat trickling down his brow.

"*Too* close," Stretch said shakily.

Enoch decided against obliging his boss; he descended by way of the ladder and advanced to repeat his apology.

"Awful sorry. Sure beg your pardon."

"You're an idiot — a dangerous idiot!" stormed Engle.

"Take it easy." Larry was regaining his composure. "Accidents happen."

"Friend, I appreciate your patience, but I got to get rid of this whelp anyway," growled Engle. "Hell, I just can't afford having him around. He's a Jonah — the worst kind of trouble. Young Hesky, get your butt out of here — *now!* You're all through!"

"I'm going — I'm going . . . " Enoch mumbled, scuttling out.

Engle tugged the pitchfork free; he was still trembling.

"Damn and blast. Nothing like that ever happened in my place before, take my word."

"Don't worry about it," soothed Larry. "Bad scare, but all over now."

Sighing heavily, the taller drifter thumbed his hat off his brow and mumbled, "I've never called myself purty but, oh hell, I don't want to *think* of what that thing would've done to my kisser."

"So forget it," urged Larry. He showed the livery-owner an amiable grin as they began offsaddling. "Feed and water and a rubdown, okay?"

"Your animals'll get the best care," said Engle, nodding distractedly. "Hell's sakes, that Hesky whelp, I can't understand why he's still alive, why he hasn't killed himself by now. Born clumsy, makes a hash of every job he tries his hand at."

"How about a hotel?" asked Larry. "You got a suggestion?"

"Bromley's" offered Engle. "A block uptown, other side of the street."

"Just in case we leave early tomorrow," offered Stretch, fishing out a coin.

While the newcomers were checking into the Bromley Hotel, Enoch was entering the building that was home and workplace to his uncle by the rear door. This put him in the kitchen under the wary gaze of his aunt. Long-suffering, well-accustomed to the misadventures of her inept nephew, Dorrie Torvill guessed aloud, "Finished at the Engle stable already?"

"Got fired, Aunt Dorrie," he shrugged. "Didn't last long, did I?"

"What's to become of you?" she wondered.

His sleeping place was a lean-to built onto the laundry adjoining the kitchen. The Torvills' quarters were upstairs, a bedroom and parlor. In his room, such as it was, he hunkered to remove old editions of the Madden County newspaper from a bottom drawer of the dresser. Finding the issue of interest to him, he reached for a pencil and squatted on his cot. The front page featured a second-hand report of a half-year-old incident in which two famous outlaw-fighters had figured, complete with photographs. He folded the paper, set it on his knees and, after inspecting it intently, pencilled mustaches and short beards onto familiar faces. By the time he had finished, there was no doubt in his mind.

'Them — nothing surer. Am I the only one knows who they are? Could be. In those fine town clothes and beards, not riding a sorrel and pinto, they do look different — except for their height of course.'

He returned the newspaper to the drawer and, for a while, pondered the significance of his discovery. Well, could there be any question as to why the heroes of his schooldays had come here? No doubt at all, not as far as he was concerned. The Duval gang's last crime had been committed right here in Maddenville. Larry Valentine and Stretch Emerson were after the Duval gang. Why else would they come here? Information, clues, a lead, some hint as to the gang's whereabouts, was what they would seek in Maddenville.

Time for him to make his move, he decided. His only chance of winning the bounty posted on Blanco Jack would be to run him down before the experts from Texas flushed him out. Had he not hunted game, and successfully? Certainly. He could follow deer tracks, so why not horse tracks, horses carrying outlaws?

Leave at sundown, he urged himself. Fine. He had time to declare his intentions to the object of his affections and, boy oh boy, would *she* be impressed! Yes, he would tell Imogene in person, but not his uncle and aunt; better to just leave them a note and sneak out of town quietly.

He hoped, as he approached the general store a short time later, to find

Imogene alone, as her father was yet another ex-employer of his and did not exactly approve of him. Too much to hope for. When he sashayed in dressed for riding and toting his Winchester, Hugh Cottrell was right there with his daughter.

"Careful with that weapon, boy," was the storekeeper's non-greeting.

"Excuse me, Mister Cottrell," frowned Enoch. "I admit I'm clumsy in some ways . . . "

"In a *lot* of ways," Cottrell corrected.

" . . . but I do know how to handle my rifle," declared Enoch. He doffed his floppy-brimmed hat and aimed a grin at auburn-haired, pretty as a picture Imogene. "Hallo, Imogene, I have great news for you."

"I'm sure nothing you say would be of interest to me, Enoch Averill Hesky," she replied haughtily.

"But I'll be riding out soon," he pleaded. "And I can't say how long I'll be gone."

"Your uncle and aunt — every citizen

of Maddenville — would be mighty happy if you *never* come back," growled Cottrell.

"But *you'll* miss me, won't you, Imogene?" he asked.

"Give me one good reason," the girl challenged.

"You'll be proud of me when I come back," he assured her.

"The conceit of him!" she remarked to her father.

"Hesky the wonder boy," jibed Cottrell.

"I'm not even slightly curious about where you're going nor why," she informed Enoch.

"Well, I'll tell you anyway." He squared his shoulders. "I'm headed into South Dakota and I aim to track down Blanco Jack Duval and nail him by golly and earn that bounty, a whole five thousand dollars."

The storekeeper clapped hand to brow and exclaimed, "Now I've heard everything!"

"You really are foolish, Enoch,"

chided Imogene. "You've failed at every task, you can't hold *any* job, so how on earth could you hope to succeed as a bounty hunter?"

"I got just one thing going for me," Enoch said resolutely. "I'm good with my rifle."

"You're too stupid to ever find Duval anyway, and just as well," said Cottrell. "It'd be the death of you — not that you'd be any loss."

"I think you're terribly foolish," scoffed Imogene.

"The die is cast," announced Enoch. "I've made my decision and there'll be no turning back."

With that, he marched out to the accompaniment of Cottrell's derisive laughter.

After he closed up for the day, Gus Torvill repaired to the kitchen for his supper and was handed the note his wife had found on their nephew's cot. He read it and waxed incredulous.

"Says he won't come back till he's collected the reward on Jack Duval."

"I read it, Gus," said Dorrie.

"Young lunatic," he growled.

"I don't wish the boy any harm," she frowned. "But maybe he'll get lost and never find his way back to Maddenville. Oh, Gus, wouldn't that be a mercy?"

"Certainly would," he agreed. "Mercy's what we deserve after two years of him on our hands — driving us crazy."

After supper at the Bromley Hotel, the trouble-shooters strolled toward the Broken Arrow.

"We'll learn somethin' we can use," Stretch predicted, always the optimist.

"Yeah, I'm feelin' lucky too," muttered Larry. "It don't have to be much, just a chance word or two, just somethin' that'll spark a hunch."

"That's all we need for starters," opined Stretch. "We've done it before, runt."

En route, they passed O'Gorman's other deputy. Luke Harroway spared them only a casual glance, to their great satisfaction. Their's could not be called an elaborate disguise, but it was working.

Entering the Broken Arrow, they approved what they saw and felt, the look of the place and its atmosphere. Townsmen patronized the Stedman establishment to relax, enjoy a few drinks and play the games of chance, not to wrangle, not to become drunk and disorderly.

They appreciated the contrast. In no way did the Broken Arrow remind them of Nader's Saloon in Varney.

3

Germ of a Hunch

AFTER they separated, Larry making for a vacant chair at a poker table, Stretch bought a double shot of rye, swapped small talk with barkeep Floyd Cooney a while, then dawdled around the games of chance. No sense rushing things. The night was young.

Stedman, bulky and dapper, presided at the poker party joined by Larry. The other players were local businessmen except for one Pardoe, another stranger in town. Larry concentrated on play, but threw in a comment or two during conversations. No need for him to be on his guard, he sensed; no sharpers in this party.

Between hands, the recent outrage was discussed. It was obvious to

Larry the victims, the hapless Steve Drummond and the manager now making a slow recovery from a gunshot wound, were popular locals.

"Helluva thing," the player to Larry's left remarked. "What a way for Drummond to go, and him one of the nicest fellers around."

"Trash, all of 'em, Duval and his kind," scowled Stedman. "Widow-makers. Cards?"

"Two for me," requested Larry. "Bad bunch, the Duval gang. I don't know a whole lot about 'em, never heard of 'em till I came to Maddenville."

"I think Duval's an albino," Stedman said in disgust.

"No, he's pale-haired but not pink-eyed," argued another player. "Got light blue eyes, it says on the bulletins."

The man on Larry's left won that hand and threw in another remark.

"Drummond in his grave and Ellis laid up and all for what? The bank was busy that day, mostly withdrawals I hear tell. Ellis calculated they got away with not much than forty-five hundred."

"Some getaway," grouched the man at Larry's right. "Real heroes, I don't think, using people as shields so O'Gorman and the deputies couldn't get a shot at 'em. And one of 'em Mattie Price. Good woman like her, a nerve case now."

"Outlaws just don't care," complained the player at Larry's left. "They hit a town like ours, no skin off their noses how much grief they cause."

"Trash," snorted Stedman, dealing. "And now they're snug in their hide-away in the Black Hills of Dakota where no search party can find 'em, probably planning their next job."

That time around, Larry took the pot with a bluff play, holding nought but a pair of sevens. As Stedman shuffled the deck, Pardoe frowned and declared, "That puzzles me — puzzles me plenty."

"What?" Stedman asked while dealing.

"What you said — what everybody

says about the Duval gang's hideout in the Black Hills," said Pardoe. "Look, on my way here, I travelled clear through the Black Hills. Still a lot of mining there, I mean a *lot* of mining, lone prospectors working claims or whole bunches of diggers working together. And the camps, places like Bowdrey's Mound, Limbo Gulch, the Fortuna camp — which is like a village — and New Start Basin and all the others."

The man at Larry's right inspected his hand and asked, "Friend, you ever getting round to making your point?"

"I'm opening," said Pardoe, nudging chips to the centre of the table. "My point? *This* is my point. With so much activity in the hills, how could Duval and his men — ten of 'em, last I heard — come and go without somebody noticing? It'd have to be some helluva hideout."

"According to our local newspaper, more than one posse has checked the hills," said Stedman.

"How *could* the gang hide there?" challenged Pardoe.

Casually, Larry asked, "The Dakota law's takin' too much for granted?"

"That's my guess." Pardoe nodded emphatically. "Plain enough they hole up *somewhere*. But, if I were heading up a search party, I'd pass up the Black Hills. I was in no hurry, you know? Overnighted at quite a few mine camps, and I can tell you no shovel-stiff, no fossicker knew anything about a hideout. The only time they saw Duval's face was on Wanted posters."

"Cards?" asked Stedman.

"I'll stay with these," decided Pardoe.

Stretch had a lucky night, won $50 at the dice table and picked up $75 playing roulette. At 11 p.m., when they left the Broken Arrow, Larry too had boosted their bankroll by $150.

"We'll he headed into Dakota manana," he announced as they walked to the hotel. "Early breakfast, then we get movin' again."

"You got somethin'," guessed Stretch.

"Ain't much, but it's worth thinkin' about," said Larry.

"Tell you all about it while we're beddin' down."

In their room, while they prepared to call it a day, he repeated the notions expressed by traveller Pardoe, his partner hanging on his every word. Having said it all, Larry patiently waited for his reaction. He hung his clothes, squatted on his bed to remove his boots while Stretch undressed slowly, his brow wrinkled.

"I'm thinkin'," he said.

"Bueno," approved Larry. "We ought never quit doin' *that*."

"Rememberin' back to all the owl-hoots we've tangled with, I recall some of the places they holed up," muttered Stretch. "Sometimes they were all towners. By day, they ran stores or livery stables or whatever. By night, they rid out to raise hell. Nobody *knew* they were bandidos."

"Right," nodded Larry.

"Sometimes it's a rundown cattle

spread, sometimes a big ranch," Stretch reminded him. "It ain't always a far-out basin or a box canyon."

"So maybe we won't even see the Black Hills," said Larry.

"Might find ourselves checkin' home-steads in lonesome places, somethin' like that. Anyway, first thing we have to do is ford Madden Creek. Dakota border's only a mile east of it. After so long, we ain't gonna cut sign of Duval's bunch, but we know they made their getaway east."

"So," said Stretch. "Dakota, here we come."

"Kill the lamp," yawned Larry.

They made a quiet departure after an early breakfast next morning. In Maddenville, they had been ignored by local rowdies and Sheriff O'Gorman and his deputies were none the wiser, completely unaware two free riders of formidable reputation had spent a night there. Well, it did happen sometimes. They did not mix into a ruckus in every town they visited. Just most of them.

Fording the creek around 10 a.m., they prowled its east bank an hour or more. Eventually they found a rock-littered section, hard, sandy ground on which hoofprints would be visible only till the next strong wind or when the creek washed its banks. "Like you said," remarked Stretch.

"Uh huh," grunted Larry. "No chance we'd cut their sign."

They rode on eastward, level with the stage route and with the bulk of the Black Hills breaking the north skyline. Not until a quarter after high noon, when Stretch's belly began growling, did they rule it was time for them to seek a site for spelling their horses and rustling up lunch. They had, as was their habit, paused at intervals to collect firewood. There was enough of it being dragged by Stretch, secure in the tightened loop of his lariat, when they came to a spring by a rock overhang, enough of it for cooking a meal and boiling coffee. Did drifting gamblers carry lariats? Maybe not, but there was one piece of equipment neither Texan would dream of leaving back in Castleton. Their range clothes, sure, their distinctive sorrel and pinto, sure. But their ropes? Never.

Stretch elected to break out provisions and get a cookfire started while Larry saw to the feeding and watering of the horses. Soon, they were hunkering by the fire, waiting for their coffeepot to start bubbling and savoring the aromas rising from the skillet. And assuming they had this whole region to themselves, until . . .

It was a distant sound, the rifle shot, then the second shot. But every triggered bullet has to end its flight somewhere unless it hurtles through space till it spends itself. That first slug didn't spend itself. It kicked grit off the top of the overhang and ricocheted, whining like a banshee above the Texans' heads. They cursed lustily and swiftly changed position, darting to their dumped gear to unsheathe their Winchesters.

"Sonofabitch!" scowled Stretch.

"We stay low — we keep our eyes peeled," growled Larry.

"That long gun's somewheres north of us."

"Somethin' *had* to happen — somethin' like this," grouched Stretch. "Life's been too quiet for us since we quit Varney with Dex Beech."

"I've heard it said there's no rest for the wicked," complained Larry. "Hell, we'd have to be the wickedest hombres . . . "

They waited, eyes narrowed, ears cocked. Several minutes passed, then the taller Texan cursed again, this time softly.

"Headed right for us. One rider."

"He's seen our smoke — 'less he's blind," muttered Larry.

He listened for a while. "Sure takin' his time."

"Yup, comin' on slow and easy," nodded Stretch.

As well as the slow plodding of hooves, they now heard tuneless whistling. One thing could be said for the approaching horseman; he was not trying to advance on them stealthily.

A few moments later the rider came into clear view — and was recognized.

"*Him* again!" scowled Larry.

The youth on the sprightly black colt had sheathed his rifle. He held his reins in his left hand. From the right dangled his kill, a jackrabbit, by one leg. Cheerily, he called to the grim-faced men rising and discarding their Winchesters.

"Well, howdy there! Good to see you gents again! Remember me?"

When he reined up, Larry coldly assured him, "We ain't apt to forget a two-legged jackass that let go of a doggone pitchfork while he was swingin' it."

"Well — uh — I already apologized for that," frowned Enoch.

"Beg our pardon again — sharpshooter," growled Larry. "One of your slugs reached us." He jerked a thumb. "Ricocheted off the top of the overhang and came too close for comfort."

"Holy cow!" exclaimed Enoch. "When I flushed those jackrabbits, I was so far away I couldn't even see your smoke — honestly!"

"I guess we can take his word for that," Stretch suggested.

"I guess," shrugged Larry.

"I hardly ever miss," Enoch assured them as he dismounted.

"Had both those critters in my sights when they cut across a rise. Missed the first one. The other one's my lunch. Share it with you if you like. Didn't sight your smoke till I started this way. Figured somebody was noon-camped and they'd let me share their fire."

"All right, you can roast your meat on our fire," said Larry. "But, when you skin and gut that rabbit . . . "

"Hold your damn knife real careful, boy," ordered Stretch.

Enoch looked to the comfort of his pony and, when he hunkered to prepare his lunch, tried big-noting himself. For a while, the veteran nomads were more amused than irritated, even a touch wistful. He was so young, so cocky. In some ways, he reminded them of the kind of youngsters they were, younger than Enoch, come to think of it, way back when they had absconded from school to enlist in the Confederate Cavalry.

Soon, they did become exasperated; the boy didn't seem to know when to stop bragging — and lying.

"I'm older than I look," he told them. "Going on twenty-two in fact. Name's Enoch Hesky . . . "

"I remember that's what the livery-owner in Maddenville called you," frowned Larry. "Hesky, huh? I could've sworn he said Pesky. It sure fits."

"My Uncle Gus, Gus Torvill the barber, bought Blackie for me," Enoch continued, gesturing to the colt. "But not my rifle. I won my Winchester last Fourth of July. Somebody lent me a rifle and, by golly, I beat every other man in the shooting contest and that beautiful Winchester was first prize.

Been odd-jobbing around Maddenville, but I'm through with all that."

"Gonna be a hunter now," guessed Stretch.

"Man hunter — bounty hunter," grinned Enoch. He fixed chunks of meat to a stick and began roasting them. "I plan on tracking down Blanco Jack Duval for the price on his head."

The Texans traded glances. Larry refrained from comment until they and the youth were eating.

"Bounty huntin's a dangerous business," he said. "Outlaws wanted dead or alive don't surrender without makin' a fight of it."

"Mostly a fight to the death," warned Stretch.

"Well, I know you famous gents never bothered much about bounty," Enoch mumbled while muching. "You fight outlaws just because you don't like for badmen to get away with murder and robbery. I sure admire you for that, Mister Valentine, Mister Emerson. But me now, I need a stake, and five thousand bucks is gonna be mighty useful to me."

They glowered at him.

"What'd you call us?" Larry coldly challenged.

"Hey, I didn't let on to anybody else," the youth hastened to assure him. "Why, I bet I'm the only Maddenville man knows you and your partner passed through town."

"Runt, I'd swear them tin stars didn't know us," frowned Stretch. "So how'd this sprig catch onto us?"

"He's about to tell us," growled Larry.

"Didn't recognize you right off — just got curious," Enoch said placatingly. "Used to read about you a lot. Liked reading about you, so I kept old newspapers. I just sketched whiskers onto a picture of you. Didn't expect I'd ever see you rigged like sporting men, but I guess you got your reasons. Anyway, your secret's safe with me."

"It better be," breathed Stretch.

"You got my word I didn't tell

anybody," offered Enoch.

"Didn't come looking for you either. Only found you accidentally. Listen, if I'm with you while others are around, what're you calling yourselves?"

"Waco Webb," said Larry.

"Brazos Billy Terhune," said Stretch.

"You can rely on me," declared Enoch. "I'm no blabbermouth." When he had eaten his fill and the Texans' plates were empty, he produced a tin cup and asked could they spare some coffee. Larry reached for the pot, Stretch for a bottle. The three cups were set in a row. Larry two-thirds filled them, remarking.

"My partner and me like our coffee spiked."

"Me too," Enoch said promptly. "I'm a man takes his booze any way it comes."

Stretch pulled the cork and generously spiked all three cups. He and Larry sipped theirs and watched. After one gulp, Enoch turned red, shuddered and began coughing frantically. Hot liquid spilled from his cup. The Texans let him suffer a few moments. Larry then took the cup, emptied it and refilled it from the pot. Came now some hard talk.

"We don't like liars," he said grimly. "And who'd you think you were foolin' anyway? If you're goin' on twenty-two, Stretch and me are goin' on eighteen."

"You don't have fuzz enough to shave yet," sneered Stretch.

"If we checked your gear, we wouldn't find no razor."

"For my money, you ain't a day older'n fifteen," jibed Larry.

"I'm sixteen!" Enoch impulsively blurted out. He cringed from their accusing stares, downed a mouthful of coffee. "Look, I'm sorry I lied about my age . . . "

"Gonna beg our pardon for all the braggin' too?" drawled Stretch.

"Yeah, that too," sighed Enoch. "And I admit — uh — I can be kind of clumsy . . . "

"You might's well admit it," Larry said mercilessly. "We ain't about to forget that damn pitchfork."

"Will you listen, give me a chance to say my piece?" begged Enoch.

"Depends," warned Larry. "I don't know if you're gonna say anything we want to hear."

"You must be hunting the Duval gang," muttered Enoch. "Why else would the Texas Trouble-Shooters be travelling this territory? You got to let me stay with you. Don't get mad, let me finish, listen to my promises." They were glowering again, but he pressed on. "First, I'll never lie to you again. Second, I'll follow your orders, Mister Valentine."

"You think we'd let a dumb kid tag along with us?" growled Stretch.

"Is that how they talked to you?" Enoch quickly countered. "The enlistment officer back when you joined the Southern Cavalry, the older horse soldiers you rode and fought with all through the war? Were you my age when you enlisted?"

The tall men grimaced, frustrated, sharing the same thought. If they ordered young Hesky to return to Maddenville, he would only pretend to do so, he would undoubtedly follow them. Larry drained his cup, lit a cigar and began some hard talking.

He led off by repeating Dex Beech's account of the tragedy that had befallen Diamond B, then declared, "My partner and me don't care spit about no reward. We're in this to fix Duval and his gunhawks one way or another. If we can, we'll take 'em alive and dump 'em on the nearest law authority. It'll be risky as hell, but we're used to riskin' our lives. Can you claim *you* are? If we take you with us, there'll be rough times and plenty danger, the kind we've faced before — but you haven't."

"You've never killed a man, kid," said Stretch.

"You don't know how it feels, havin'

to return fire to protect yourself," muttered Larry.

"Jackrabbits can't shoot back at you," Stretch pointed out. "Bandidos always do."

"And we mightn't find Duval at all," said Larry. "Forget what you've read about us. We can't work miracles and, right now, we got no notion where the gang's holed up."

"I won't be a burden on you," pleaded Enoch. "Maybe I'll be nervous when the time comes, but not so scared I'd cut and run. Give me a chance. I have to grow up just like you did."

Stretch drew a blazing twig from the fire to light a stogie. He eyed Enoch dubiously and asked, "What d'you think, runt?"

"Too early to say," Larry said irritably. "We ain't even started to test him."

"So test me," urged Enoch. "Come on, make me show you."

"You got shells for your rifle?" demanded Larry.

"Magazine's full except for the two slugs I triggered at the rabbits, and I got maybe eight spares," answered Enoch.

"And you won a shootin' contest — shootin' at fixed targets, right?" frowned Larry. The youth nodded eagerly. "Good, but not good enough, not if we get into a gunfight. A movin' man blastin' at you is no fixed target." He nodded to Stretch. "Help yourself to the field-glasses. Maybe you can climb atop the overhang. You might see a long way from up there and, testin' this sassy hot shot, we better be sure no peaceable pilgrim stops a wild one."

Unhurriedly, Stretch rose, went to his partner's gear for the binoculars, then moved to the overhang. While he was climbing, Enoch cheerily assured Larry, "No danger I'll slow you down." He made to rise. "Want me to show you how fast Blackie can run?"

"Siddown." Exasperated, Larry declared, "No need. I look at your horse, I *know* he's fast." He puffed on his cigar and patted the butt of his Colt. "You any use with a hogleg?"

"Just with my rifle," said Enoch. "I never fooled with pistols. Figured I should rely on the weapon I savvy best."

A few minutes later, Stretch descended to rejoin them and report, "Nary a soul in sight."

"All right." Larry nodded to Enoch. "On your feet, and bring your rifle along."

Enoch walked with the Texans some forty yards east of the campsite. When they paused, Stretch pointed to a log from which three feet of dead branch jutted upward.

"Over there, runt."

"Oh huh, I see it," grunted Larry. "Kid . . . ?"

"I see it," said Enoch. "You mean the old branch poking up from that . . . ?"

"It's a staked out Duval man aimin' a handgun at you," said Larry. "No, don't cock till I tell you. You ain't spotted him yet, don't know he's there till I say 'now', savvy? Look away and wait. When I give you the word, *then* you cock and get your shot off. It's him or you, understand?"

"All right," said Enoch.

Larry worked his stogie to the side of his mouth.

"Now," he said sharply.

It seemed to happen in one swift series of movements, Enoch levering a shell into his breech as he half-turned, firing one-handed, the stock of his Winchester steadied against his right hip. With the bark of the report, the dead branch was severed. The Texans were grudgingly impressed.

"Hey, how about that?" grinned Enoch.

"What're you waitin' for — applause?" Larry asked sourly. "Room enough back of that log to hide two of 'em. By now, the second hombre'd be blowin' a hole through you."

Without waiting to be asked, the taller Texan ambled back to the campfire. When he reappeared, he brought with him an empty bean-can.

"I read your mind," he told Larry.

"Yeah, fine," said Larry, his eyes on Enoch. "Listen now. Stretch'll throw it high." He swept back his coattails. "When I hit it, you won't know whichaway it's gonna fly, up, down, left or right. You have to hit it after *I* hit it, savvy? Go on. This time you can cock first."

Enoch levered another shell into his breech, working by feel, trying to watch both Texans simultaneously. Stretch hurled the can high and Larry's Colt seemed to leap into his hand. His gun arm swung upward, the six-shooter boomed and the target careered away at an angle. Enoch raised his rifle, sighted and fired and, as the can's flight was diverted by his bullet, he recocked, fired again and hit it again before it fell to the ground.

Enoch's triumphant grin faded. Larry was talking grimly while ejecting his spent shell and reloading and holstering his Colt, and Stretch was moving closer to contribute his own statements.

"You have to be that fast, that straight, while your target's shootin' at you," warned Larry.

"Ever feel the wind of a slug fannin' your ear?" challenged Stretch. "It ain't good, kid."

"Somebody scores on you, creases you or puts a bullet in your leg," said Larry. "So you're down, but you don't dare just flop there. You got to roll, keep movin', try for another bead on him because it's for sure he'll take another shot at you."

"Even if you're only creased, it hurts the worst way, burns like a red-hot brand," Stretch said relentlessly. Enoch was recoiling, blinking uneasily. "You got pain, but you can't pay it no mind."

"Can't afford to even think of the pain, because there ain't time!" snapped Larry. "You keep on shootin' straight as you can. You're caught up in a gunfight, so that's the only chance you've got!"

"We've been there, boy, so we *know*," growled Stretch.

"Nothin' noisier'n a gunfight, nothin' so messy," Larry impressed on him. "There's gunsmoke and there's blood on the ground and it ain't purty."

"It's never fun," declared Stretch.

"Only way you stay alive is make sure the other hombre don't," scowled Larry.

They fell silent, dropping their cigar stubs, grinding them under their heels and watching Enoch's face. When he found his voice, he spoke quietly, no hint of conceit nor defiance.

"I promise — I won't forget anything you've said."

"So what d'you say, runt?" prodded Stretch. "He stayin' with us?"

"Ask me when I'm through testin' him," said Larry. He stood scanning the area east a moment, then decided, "Time to break camp and, for the rest of today, we'll ride the regular trail."

"Returning to the overhang, they refilled their canteens at the spring, killed the fire and packed all gear. Soon, they were in the saddle and on the move again, and Enoch well realized it was too early for him to congratulate himself on becoming a sidekick of the case-hardened outlaw-fighters. He had demonstrated his skill with a Winchester, but this was only the start of it. Until now he had believed Larry to be the tougher of the two, short on patience, a cynic and a sceptic, and Stretch the easy-going one, an indulgent soft touch.

It wasn't working out that way. He had been warned of what could be in store for him, not only by Larry but by a just-as-grim Stretch. So be it. He was learning. To win the approval of his heroes, he would have to subdue his high spirits, pay attention to every command and break down on the brashness.

Toward sundown, they had reached an area thickly-timbered. Finding firewood would be no problem and, for an overnight camp, the Texans chose a shallow, rock-ringed hollow in sight of the timber and some fifty yards from the stage trail.

Again, the taller drifter elected himself cook and made short work of building a fire and selecting provisions while his partner, aided by Enoch now, took care of the horses. During that meal, the youth was questioned about his background. He gave truthful answers, acknowledging the late Abraham and Zelda Hesky had been good parents, assuring his interrogators he duly appreciated being taken in by his uncle and aunt and making no attempt to excuse his clumsiness and past failures.

"I guess being good with my Winchester's my only real talent," he offered. "No more bragging — I promised. Maybe it comes naturally or maybe it's because I practice a lot. I wish I was good at all kinds of other things, but that's how it goes."

"He savvies horses too, runt," remarked Stretch.

"If he was no use around horses, I wouldn't've let him come this far with us," Larry said bluntly.

"I'll keep doing my best," vowed Enoch.

"Your best better be good enough," retorted Larry. "From here on, whenever we night-camp, one of us stays awake and sits guard while the others sleep."

"I'll do my share," said Enoch.

"Damn right you will," said Stretch.

"After we're through eatin', Stretch and me gonna catch up on our shut-eye," announced Larry. "You'll sit first guard. That means you squat by the rim of this hollow, keep your eyes peeled and your ears cocked, Savvy? Come midnight, if one of us has to rouse you, there'll be some ass-kickin' — you got that? And you'll be finished with us. When a man keeps watch, he ain't just guardin' the horses. He's responsible for the lives of them he's travellin' with."

"When you're relieved, kid, you'd

better be wide awake and with your eyes open," advised Stretch. "No matter how weary you get, keep them eyes open, hear?"

"Midnight might seem a long time from now," said Larry. "If you get to yawnin', feel like you can't hold out till midnight, don't flop or close your eyes, not even for a minute. Come wake one of us."

"All right, I think I can stay sharp till midnight," nodded Enoch.

Larry gave him his watch.

"Take good care of that. I'm kind of attached to it."

"Sure," said Enoch.

He was fortunate, not yet drowsy when, a few minutes before midnight, Larry rose, threw more wood on the fire and came to the rim to relieve him and retrieve his timepiece.

"Haven't been catnapping, cross my heart," mumbled Enoch, rising stiffly. "By golly, it's quiet hereabouts. I didn't even hear a coyote wail."

"Bunk down," Larry gruffly ordered.

He assumed correctly that the youngster would be in dreamland seconds after rolling into his blanket by the fire. Sitting crosslegged with his rifle resting across his knees, he scanned the moonlit terrain and admitted to himself that his decision was made.

It would not be the first time the trouble-shooters had sought a dangerous foe with a third party, sometimes female, tagging along. Clumsy though he was, pitifully immature in many ways, the kid might just prove useful. And, as on other such occasions, there was that aggravating possibility the trouble-shooters could not ignore, the possibility that, if rejected, the third party would tag them at a distance. That had happened before.

He thought of all the others and wondered. 'Why do they do it? When'll they learn men like us are dangerous company? Hell, we got our hands full takin' care of ourselves without havin' to look out for a damn greenhorn.'

He did not and never would consider

the heroworship aspect because, like his partner, he never thought of himself as the hero type. The drifters had their failings. Conceit was not one of them.

In the after midnight hours, he let his mind drift back to Varney and the journey with Dex Beech, the pain in Beech's eyes and three graves in the Pegrum County cemetery, last resting place of his wife Madeline and sons Richard and Hollis. Merciless they were and contemptuous of their victims and the kin of their victims, Duval and his men and most of the other desperadoes challenged and fought by the Texas Trouble-Shooters. And so, when it came to the showdown, how much mercy would *they* deserve? It would be kill or be killed, nothing surer.

Around quarter of four, with his eyelids heavy, he roused Stretch and flopped by the fire again. When he woke to the sunlight, the fire had been built up and his partner was fixing breakfast. Enoch stirred, sitting up, knuckling at his eyes.

"Quiet night, huh runt?" Stretch remarked.

"Dead quiet," nodded Larry. "But how many more quiet nights will we have? Quien sabe?"

"You got firewood enough?" asked Enoch. "Want me to . . . ?"

"Got all we need," said Stretch.

From his canteen, the youth poured just enough water into a cupped hand to clear his eyes. He then enquired, after some hesitation, "Have I passed your tests?"

"You can come along with us," frowned Larry, "for as long as you remember Rule One."

"Rule One." Enoch nodded understandingly. "Do as I'm told."

"That's it," said Larry.

Later that day, following the east trail, they noted they were drawing closer to the southern reaches of the Black Hills. Another fifteen minutes brought them to a turn-off leading north and a signpost showing a name Larry had heard mentioned in Maddenville.

"Limbo Gulch," he mused.

"That Pardoe feller told you of it, you said," Stretch recalled.

"Uh huh," grunted Larry. "One of a lot of mine camps in this high country. I got no reason to disbelieve what Pardoe said about the Black Hills. Ain't likely Duval would hole up there. But the sign says we could make it before sundown, and maybe they got a saloon. It's gettin' hot. We could use a cold beer."

"We gonna overnight there?" asked Stretch.

"If we can find a place to bunk," decided Larry.

"Hotel," guessed Enoch. "Might be a hotel."

"But, if there ain't no hotel, we might's well come on back to this trail and find us another campin' place," suggested Stretch.

"Sure," nodded Larry. "It just depends what we find in Limbo Gulch."

After they swung onto the turn-off

to follow the narrower trail north, the taller Texan voiced a hunch.

"No use us askin' questions about the Duval gang."

"But maybe there'll be talk of 'em," opined Larry. "And we can always listen."

It was still daylight when they sighted Limbo Gulch, and first impressions weren't encouraging.

4

Arrival and Departure

THE Texans had seen other such mine camps but, for young Enoch, Limbo Gulch was a new experience. Riding in slowly three abreast, they took in all there was to see. Shafts had been bored into the slanting rock walls east and west of the gulch floor. There were log and clapboard buildings, only two of them, the Pay Lode Hotel and the saloon, double-storeyed. There were also tents, lean-tos and tarpaper shacks, a town marshal's office with a small jail in back, a livery stable and, closer at hand on their left, the premises of Jethro Morcombe, a carpenter doubling as undertaker. They saw no stagecoach depot, no telegraph office, no schoolhouse, and nothing remotely resembling a place of worship. Could a traveller buy a meal here? Maybe the Pay Lode boasted a dining-room, or maybe the unimpressive Dodd's Cafe served passable food.

They were hailed as they drew level with the marshal's office, so reined up to be appraised by the shabby, unshaven badge-toter. He identified himself as Ezra Purl, the town marshal, and curtly asked, "Lose your way?"

Larry shook his head and gestured northward.

"Headed through the hills clear to Deadwood," he offered.

"Might overnight here if we can find a little action. Like you've guessed, gamblin's our business."

"I'm the only law here," Purl informed them. "So I got to check on strangers. Who are you?"

"They call me Waco Webb," said Larry. "My partner here, he's Brazos Billy Terhune. And the kid? That's all he's called. Just Kid."

"Sportin' men, huh?" mumbled Purl.

"Well, no crooked play at the saloon, Goldie Covett's. She don't hold with sharpers. Pay Lode Hotel's fairly comfortable — only hotel here anyway."

For once, Stretch took the initiative, but to his partner's approval.

"Sure hope this camp's peaceful, Marshal. We hear tell Blanco Jack Duval's outfit's still on the loose. We're leery of trouble so, if he raids Limbo Gulch, we'd like it to be after we're gone."

"No bank here," replied Purl. "Duval likes banks. And, if he came raidin' for whatever gold's been mined herein, him and his bunch'd never get out alive. Every man'd fort up to fight 'em off and keep what's his. No." He shook his head vehemently. "This ain't the kinda town Blanco Jack'd risk hittin.'"

"We're mighty relieved to hear that," declared Larry. "Be seein' you, Marshal."

They ambled their mounts a short distance along the rutted area between the Gulch's shabby buildings and paused for a parley. Other denizens of the camp had them under observation, all of them in the rough garb of prospectors. Enoch softly confided, "I won't be sleeping all night at the hotel. After supper, I think I'll sneak to the stable and bunk in the hayloft."

"Somethin' spokin' you?" challenged Stretch.

"Yeah," nodded Enoch. "I'm leery of the way some of those jaspers're looking Blackie over. They got greedy eyes and, next to my rifle, he's the most valuable thing I own. If I lost him . . . "

"All right, we'll stable our critters now," muttered Larry. "And let's act natural. We're just three travellers passin' through, okay?"

Still under observation, they moved on to the livery stable. As they led their animals in, a skinny, wall-eyed man rose from a stool, studied them in a sullen way and growled, "Dollar a night. Take it or leave it."

Enoch frowned uneasily, but the Texans were expert at tight-reining their feelings; they showed no resentment.

"It's your barn, friend," shrugged Larry.

He paid the $3, after which they unslung their gear, offsaddled their horses and put them in stalls. The stable-owner stood by, making no move to help them.

From the stable, they hefted their gear and walked back to the hotel. Their reception there was no more cordial. The double-chinned, balding proprietor charged them $5 apiece for an overnight stay in three singles upstairs. There was no register to be signed and, after parting with $15, Larry had to ask for keys. The hotel-owner grimaced impatiently, but handed him three keys.

"No dinin' room here," he growled. "Only place you can eat is the hash-house, Dodd's."

"You kin to the nice feller runs the livery stable?" Stretch enquired.

"What?" frowned the hotel-owner.

"Forget I asked — friend," sighed Stretch.

They climbed the rickety stairs and unlocked three adjoining rooms. Opening the doors, they saw only the bare essentials, lumpy-looking beds, flimsy chairs, wash-basin and water pitcher, not much else.

"Get back to me soon as you're unpacked." urged Larry. "We'll pow-wow some more." Joined by his companions a few minutes later, he showed them a wry grin. "Welcome to Limbo Gulch, friendliest little town in the Black Hills."

"Maybe we oughtn't expect no better," said Stretch. "Plain enough every son's leery of strangers here, and plain enough why. They're minin' and stashin' the real stuff and they ain't lookin' to get robbed."

"You got it right," opined Larry.

"Only reason there's a stable and a hotel is to accommodate travellers bound south," suggested Enoch, "or north to Deadwood or Belle Fourche."

"That'd be right too," agreed Larry.

"Don't seem like we'll learn anything about Duval here," said Stretch.

"You never can tell," mused Larry. "Think back now. When we rode in, did you get the feelin' a lot of minders knew we were comin'?"

"I think that mean-eyed marshal was waitin' for us," frowned Stretch.

"They likely post lookouts atop the rock walls," nodded Larry. "Well, if they spotted us, maybe they've spotted the Duval gang. I don't mean up close. I mean in the distance, headed on east or maybe south. After supper, we'll take a look at Goldie's Place. Might be we'll find a miner that don't mind talkin' to strangers." Enoch coughed and shrugged self consciously. "Somethin' botherin' you, kid?"

"When you let me join up with you, I didn't mean for it to cost you," Enoch apologized. "Money, I mean. Eight dollars already, and just for a room and a stall for Blackie."

"How much dinero are you totin'?" demanded Larry.

"Not much," sighed Enoch. "About a dollar seventy-five."

"So keep it," said Larry. "For as long as you're with us, I don't reckon you'll put a big dent in our bankroll."

"We got plenty, kid," drawled Stretch. "Had plenty when we hit Maddenville, and we won an extra couple hundred there."

"Two hundred and seventy-five," said Larry, rising. "All right now, you two feelin' brave enough to risk the chow at the cafe?"

When they quit the hotel to begin the short walk to the Dodd establishment, it was near sundown. Larry noticed, but with only casual interest, a man rigged as a miner carrying two heaped plates from the cafe to Morcombe's. He thought little of this at the time. Had he been interested enough to make a guess, he might have assumed the man intended eating with the carpenter-undertaker.

Dodd proved to be only slightly more affable than the owners of the livery stable and hotel. There were only a few other diners. And the quality of the food? They had tasted better, much better, and that went double for what passed as coffee. However, Larry's nose detected no noisome odors; this was rough fare, but their chances of escaping ptomaine were probably better than even.

Outside Dodd's, they separated, the Texans making for Goldie's Place, Enoch returning to the hotel to collect his rifle, use the rear exit and wait his chance to sneak into the livery stable and hide in the hayloft.

It was as tawdry an excuse for a saloon as the drifters had ever patronized, but pretty much what they expected of Limbo Gulch's only watering hole. The bar was constructed of planks supported by barrels that had once contained beer. Mule freighters were overdue here, so there was no beer; you took your chances with the rotgut from the still out back. A couple of sips convinced the newcomers they would imbibe very little of this firewater; they were hard drinkers from way back, but they had their standards.

The place was rough and the atmosphere thick with the odors of sweating humanity, tobacco, booze and the cheap perfume of big Goldie Covett and her half-dozen bawds. No roulette layout here. At some time in the past, an upright piano had been freighted in. A derby-hatted cigar-chewer in shirtsleeves was seated at the yellowing keyboard, half-heartedly strumming 'Oh, Dem Golden slippers' on an instrument long overdue for retuning. Card tables and dice set-up were all this place offered in the way of games of chance. As for the fat, hennaed proprietress, piggy-eyed with her flesh bulging out of a green satin gown, Larry sensed her greed: her second name would have seemed more appropriate if spelt with only one T.

Purl was here, Larry observed, also

the skinny jasper from the livery stable. Nudging him, Stretch muttered, "I'll try socializin' with the miners. You'll buy into a poker game, I guess, and can you hope for a square deal in this hell-house? We don't like to be rich, runt, but you better not loose all the dinero we got."

"Well, I still got eyes to see with," shrugged Larry.

"Lotsa luck," said Stretch, drifting away.

The dapper, lynx-eyed character presiding at a poker table traded a few remarks with the fat woman as Larry approached; he heard her call him Duke. There was a spare chair. The other players, miners, nodded moodily to his request that he be allowed join them. He made himself comfortable, traded nods with Duke and play resumed.

By 10.45 p.m., Larry was in no doubt as to why he had dropped $200. If a sallow-complexioned Duke wasn't a crooked dealer, Sitting Bull wasn't a full-blood Sioux.

Sharing a table with a trio of miners, Stretch got them talking. He learned there were no wives in Limbo Gulch. All its males were single. As for the Duval gang, they had never been sighted hereabouts.

By 11 p.m., Larry had recouped his losses with two bluffplays. This seemed to cause some resentment. Duke began shuffling again and, with a bland smile, Larry drawled, "I'd take it kindly if you dealt mine from atop the deck."

"What'd you say?" frowned Duke.

"You're good and fast I'll allow, but so are my eyes," said Larry. "Let's keep the game friendly — and straight."

"I'm no sharper," snapped Duke.

"So maybe I'm mistaken," shrugged Larry. "Go ahead. Deal 'em again."

At this time, a man in miner's rig was unhurriedly approaching the livery stable, and the youth in the hayloft was wide awake and jumpy, his Winchester cocked.

The deck had been shuffled and, this

time, Larry was sure his five cards had been dealt off the top. He picked up his hand and, with his rugged face devoid of expression, put his appreciative eyes on three queens.

A miner opened the betting. Duke raised and so did Larry — a little higher. When it came time to discard, he got rid of the two of spades and the five of diamonds and was dealt the eight of hearts and the fourth queen. He upped the ante. The others pulled out, but the dealer had to be sitting behind a good hand. The pot tallied to $500 when he spread his cards face up.

"I can always smell out a bluffer," he bragged. "If your eyes're as good as you claim, you're lookin at a full house, jacks and deuces."

"I'm still takin' the pot," said Larry. "My luck runs higher when you deal square." He showed his hand. "Four ladies." He was warned by Duke's venomous glare. Delving into his coat, the dealer produced a handkerchief.

He was raising it as though to mop his brow when Larry glimpsed just a small piece of what it concealed and reacted quickly. He threw himself backward, overturning his chair just as the hideaway pistol barked. The other players hurried to get clear and Larry was on his back only for a moment, then rising with his Colt out and cocked. Duke stood braced, face contorted, the small pistol levelled at him. He took one pace to his right as he squeezed trigger and the roar of his Colt merged with the bark of the other weapon. The bullet didn't speed past his head. It bored a hole in the roof because Duke was collapsing as he fired his second shot, and now his multi-colored vest was predominantly red — blood-red.

The piano-player had dropped behind his instrument. Purl was gawking, but there were no screams from Goldie Covett and the hard-boiled bawds. And Stretch was upright, his right hand gunfilled. Grim-faced, in the sudden silence, Larry recocked his .45, out-stared the onlookers and, left-handed, transferred his winnings to a pocket.

"We don't hold with . . . " began Purl.

"C'mon, you blind?" challenged Stretch. "The dude tried for my partner with a sneak-gun."

From the hayloft, Enoch warily watched a man enter the barn and begin checking stalls. As well as his rough garb, the local wore a six-gun in a tied-down holster. He reached the black's stall, studied that fine animal a moment, then grinned and made to open it. Enoch nervously cleared his throat. The man looked up, his unprepossessing visage clear in the lamp-light.

"Hey, mister," said Enoch. "That's my horse."

The man chuckled, seeing only the face of a raw youth.

"*Used* to be yours, boy," he retorted.

He drew fast and, as far as Enoch was concerned, there was only one thing he could do. He did it fast, rising to one knee with his Winchester's muzzle dipped and spurting flame and lead. His victim fired, but a full second after the report of the rifle and with Enoch's bullet in his chest, and Enoch remembered something said by Stretch and felt his pulse race; the .45 slug had come close enough for him to feel its hot wind against his left cheek.

The two shots, clearly audible in the saloon, interrupted Purl's attempt to out-talk the Texans. He tensed. The livery owner was quickly on his feet and declaring, "Them shots come from my place!"

With Enoch on their minds, Larry and Stretch nevertheless kept their Colts cocked and their eyes wary.

"We'll go take a look over there," growled Larry. "But no hothead better forget we'll defend ourselves if we got to."

"No rash moves, gents," cautioned Stretch, sidling to the entrance with Larry.

Accompanied by Purl, the livery man and several others, they hustled across the rutted ground between the saloon and the barn. Enoch hadn't budged. The dead man had slumped to an awkward posture, gun still in hand, smoke wisping from its muzzle.

"I — I was right!" cried Enoch, as they all stared up at him. "Somebody *did* try to steal Blackie!"

"What the hell . . . ?" began Purl.

"His word's good enough for you, if you're an honest lawman," drawled Stretch.

"Use your eyes," Larry coldly invited. "It was the kid or him, and the kid's bullet ain't in his back. His iron's still in his paw — smokin'."

"I wouldn't've fired if he hadn't drawn on me," protested Enoch.

"We know that," nodded Larry. "The marshal knows it too." He eyed Purl challengingly. "Right?"

"Well, damn it . . . " growled Purl.

"It had to happen like the kid says," declared Larry.

"Marshal, we're peaceable," Stretch said gently. "But there's somethin' you better believe. You don't want trouble from us."

"Two men dead!" fumed Purl.

"Self-defense both times," countered Larry.

"Them that brings trouble ain't welcome here," scowled Purl. "You're leavin' — right now."

"Bein' the only law here, you got a right to order us out," Larry conceded. "Fine by us, but let's do it right. That badge means it's up to you to make sure there's no more gunplay. You stand by, okay? We take our horses to the hotel, pack our stuff and leave quiet and peaceful — 'less some other fool takes a shot at us."

The lawman's uncertainty intrigued both trouble-shooters. Purl gnawed at his underlip a long moment before grudgingly telling the other men, "Yeah, boys, that's how it better be."

Enoch climbed down from the loft. While he saddled the black, Larry readied his and Stretch's animals. Stretch stood by; he had holstered his Colt, but his hand was on its butt and his eyes busy. The gapers took the hint and withdrew.

Slowly, with Purl keeping pace, the saddled horses were led along to the hotel hitch-rail. Larry and the youth hurried inside, leaving the taller Texan to assure the shifty-eyed Purl, "There didn't have to be no killin' here. Wouldn't've been if the dude and the horse-thief'd kept their paws clear of their hardware."

"Uh — well — maybe so." Purl shrugged uncomfortably.

A short time later, Larry and Enoch emerged hefting packrolls, saddlebags, sheathed Winchesters and the provision-sack. One by one, they got mounted.

"Walk along with us," Larry said to Purl; it was an order, not a request.

Purl did as he was told. Slowly, with right hands brushing their holsters, the Texans and their young companion made northward with the lawman trudging beside them. Once clear of the lamp-light, they aimed casual nods at Purl, heeled the animals and travelled on, out of the gulch and up the winding trail.

"Howdy, Limbo Gulch, and adios," remarked Stretch.

"This was — a bad place for us to be," mumbled Enoch.

"No talk till we're well and truly clear," said Larry. "If a bunch of soreheads try taggin' us, I want to hear 'em comin'."

At midnight, it being obvious there would be no pursuit, the Texans slowed the pace and kept their eyes on the brush and rocks east of the trail. The moonlight was bright at this hour; they easily sighted the track cutting east off their route.

"Game-track, maybe," suggested Stretch.

"We're far enough from the Gulch, I reckon," decided Larry. "We'll try the track, travel it Injun file. What we got to do is get clear of these hills and find us a night-camp."

By following that track, they left the Black Hills behind them. The terrain east, though moonlight, offered ample cover, rock clumps aplenty and thick brush. In the early morning hours, they climbed the near slope of a timbered ridge and, from its summit, descended half-way down its eastside to a broad shelf. As good a place as any, Larry observed. They would warm themselves with a fire and, until sun-up, take turns to sit guard; the top of the ridge would be the lookout post.

As they built their fire, Larry urged the youth to speak his mind. First kill. Was he all shook up inside, about to throw up?

"Nothin' to be ashamed of, kid," soothed Stretch. "You did nothin' you didn't have to do."

"Well?" demanded Larry.

"You don't have to worry about me," sighed Enoch. "It wasn't fun — just like you warned. I guess, all of a sudden, I feel a little older."

"Man's got a right to protect what's his," Larry said gruffly. "His horse. Anything. Includin' his life."

"Yeah, I understand," nodded Enoch. "And that's how it was. He was opening Blackie's stall when I called down to him 'That's my horse.' He looked up and saw me and — I swear he laughed. '*Used* to be yours,' he said, and then he drew his gun and we both fired and — now I know how it feels — the wind of a bullet."

The tall men traded glances. They were sharing a memory, their first taste of combat — and neither of them Enoch Hesky's age at that time.

"You get any sleep up there in the hay?" asked Larry.

Enoch shook his head, but assured him, "I'm not tired. I can take the first watch."

"No," said Larry. "Sleep now. We'll wake you if you have to take over from either of us."

After the youth was rolled in his blankets by the fire, the Texans climbed to the timbered hogs-back and hunkered for a parley.

"Find out anything?" prodded Larry.

"Not much," said Stretch. "You?"

"Didn't get any chance for talk," complained Larry. "Too busy watchin' the dude's tricky hands. Not much, huh? *How* much?"

"The females we saw in that gyp-joint're the only females at the Gulch," said Stretch. "Every hombre's a bachelor and they don't know or care nothin' about the Duval bunch. Some of the miners share shacks. Dodd and Morcombe the carpenter and the galoot that runs the livery stable, they live by 'emselves." He hesitated a moment before remarking, "Too bad about the kid."

"Too bad," Larry moodily agreed.

"Wouldn't've happened if we didn't let him ride with us," frowned Stretch. "We supposed to feel guilty about that?"

Larry considered that question. Then, "I reckon not," he said. "One helluva

124

handsome cayuse, his charcoal. Any place he rides by himself there'll be trailtrash that'd kill for so fine a horse. Sooner or later, with or without us, there'd come a time he'd have to fight for his life. Next time, he'll shoot just as fast and straight, but he won't feel so squeamish."

"Uh huh," grunted Stretch. "Comes to a shootout, the squeamish're apt to get the worst of it." He settled himself, caressing his rifle. "You might's well bed down, runt. I'll rouse you if I get sleepy 'tween now and sun-up."

"All right," said Larry. "You do that."

He descended to the shelf, checked on the horses, then rolled into his blanket by the fire. On its other side, Enoch was in deep sleep, his snoring quieter, a little easier on the ears than the snuffling and trumpeting accompaniment to Emerson's slumber.

Quite a night it had been for this raw youth, he reflected. First blood. For a few moments, he anticipated he would stay awake, brooding, but soon he too was sleeping.

An hour before dawn, he roused to the feel of his partner's hand on his shoulder.

"You get on up there, runt. I'll catnap till sun-up, then fix us breakfast."

"Nothin' to see?"

"Not a damn thing. My guess is no son's budged from the gulch. They'll plant the dude and the horse-thief this mornin' and forget us."

Returning to the summit of the ridge, Larry trudged to its west edge and stared away to the distant bulk of the Black Hills. The information-seeking visit to Limbo Gulch had been fruitless, a mistake, he was thinking. To check the other camps named by Pardoe — Bowdrey's Mound, Fortuna, New Start Basin — would be just as futile. Better they should comb more of the terrain east, play his hunch the Duval gang's hideaway was an out of the way homestead or an outlying ranch.

When he rejoined his partner and the

youth for breakfast, he repeated this conviction. Stretch agreed, prediciting their quarry would be hard to find. It could take time.

"But we got plenty of that," he shrugged.

"Sure," nodded Larry. He ate for a while in silence, then suggested," Dex Beech better be a patient man."

"He'll be easier of mind when there's no more Duval gang," muttered Stretch. "Too bad it has to take so long. Still, that's how it goes. Sometimes we just stumble onto the buzzards we're huntin' couple days after we start lookin', and sometimes it takes longer."

Enoch was quiet. Delayed reaction, the Texans supposed, but he would come out of it; meanwhile, his appetite wasn't affected.

Breakfast over, they killed their fire, packed all gear and got started again, descending the ridge's east slope and taking to the somewhat cheerless terrain dead ahead. Away to the south, they could see the trail they had followed east before swinging onto the track leading to Limbo Gulch, the regular east-west stage route. They would keep it in sight, Larry decided, but would continue to travel around rockmounds and on the north side of screening brush. Instinct told him they should, until they sighted a homestead or found themselves on cattle range, keep their presence in this area a secret.

★ ★ ★

This morning, in sizeable Gould City, northeast of the land now travelled by the Texans and their young sidekick, an ill-tempered deputy sheriff whose right arm was splinted and supported by a sling made his way to his boss's office.

Phineas Judd, sheriff of Gould County, was a pipe-smoker, as was Saul Greeber, the county jailer. The lean and shrewed-eyed Judd favored a bent-stemmed brier; pudgy Greeber smoked a corncob. Judd's elder deputy, heavyset Angus Munro, still smoked the straight-stemmed meerschaum he had bought the year he was sworn in. The headquarters of law and order was smoky when the junior deputy, six-feet-two and excessively irritated by the condition of his arm, marched in and made his announcement.

"This could be the day."

With that, he flopped into a chair under the intent gaze of his elders.

"Stranger, Mike?" asked Judd.

"And no doubt a respectable-looking stranger," opined Munro with a bland grin. Scots are said to be dour, but he was of cheerful disposition and grinned a lot. "Butter wouldn't melt in his mouth?"

"Brown town suit and a derby to match," nodded Mike. "Sure he looks respectable, but I've been keepin' an eye on him and I . . . "

"He hasn't noticed you watching him I hope," said Judd.

"No, I've been mighty careful," declared Mike.

"Too bad you weren't as careful yesterday, young feller," drawled the turnkey. "Hustlin', always hustlin'. In a big hurry to mail a letter to your kin back in Texas, so what happens? You trip on the sidewalk outside of the Postal Telegraph, take a hard fall and break your doggone arm."

"You got to keep rubbin' it in, Saul?" scowled Mike.

"A good deputy is never a tanglefoot," chided Judd.

"Workin' with men twice my age can be a pain in the butt," complained Mile. "It's like I was still in school instead of a full-grown twenty-five-year-old man."

"You're repeating yourself, you say that all the time," said Judd. "Come on now, tell us all about this stranger. If you've pegged him for a Duval scout, I want to know why."

"Why," said Mike, "is because the places he's interested in· are the banks and the stage depot. Every time I spot him, that's where he's hangin' round — a bank or the stage depot."

"Mike could be right," Judd remarked to Munro.

"It's a possibility," agreed his senior deputy. "Only one of 'em identifiable, Duval himself. No descriptions on the others, so they can show up anywhere, scout around, pick up information — the kind Duval needs." He nodded and grinned, a smug grin this time. "Well, Phin, our preparations are complete. Gone to considerable pains, have we not, to set a bandit-trap?"

"Considerable pains is putting it mild," frowned Judd, glancing to the closed jailhouse door. "Those things Curly Tebbut made for us."

"Best blacksmith you'd find any-where in Dakota is Curly," muttered Greeber. "Damnedest idea I ever heard of, them contraptions."

"And I don't get to use one of 'em," grouched Mike. "It won't be me on the seat with Pete Reisner."

"No use griping, Mike," shrugged the sheriff. "No part in this deal for a one-armed lawman. Now whereabouts is he right now, this stranger?"

Mike rose and moved to the doorway to scan the street, first the south, then the north end.

"On a sidewalk bench," he reported. "Pretendin' to read a newspaper, but he's watchin' the Occidental Bank."

"Up till now, Angus, you and Dade Wakely have just been rehearsing," said Judd. "This might be the right time for a performance. If he's a spy, now's the time to find out."

"How about the shipment?" Munro asked, getting to his feet.

"Tell Dade day after tomorrow," urged Judd. "That should give Duval's spy — if that's what he is — plenty of time to pass the word. Mike, you know what you have to do."

Both deputies knew what they had to do. When Munro walked out, the morose Mike gave him a two-minute start and followed.

5

Spy Route

COUNTY sheriffs and Federal lawmen had cursed the elusive Blanco Jack Duval for a long time. Banks and stagecoaches had been looted and innocent people had been wounded or slain by the blond bandit and his heavily-armed followers. One search party after another had made wide sweeps of the areas plundered by the gang. Duval had to have a hideout; on this, every law officer was unanimous. But where? And how far can fugitives be followed when at least one of their number is expert at the fine art of killing their back-trail?

In South Dakota, there were two lawmen not content to just curse the Duval gang, and their names were Judd and Munro. For many weeks, these wily veterans had applied themselves to the planning of a strategy, not to solve the secret of the location of the bandits' hideout, but to lure them into open country, to trap and capture them.

The scheme was elaborate, but there was logic to it; the notorious Texas Trouble-Shooters weren't the only outlaw-fighters who favored shock tactics, the element of surprise.

His badge gleaming on his vest, Angus Munro strode to the Occidental Bank and entered, sparing no glance for the brown-suited lounger behind the open newspaper. When he emerged, he crossed the main street and made for the stage depot. He had aroused the stranger's curiosity. This was obvious to the younger deputy, whose vantage-point was a discarded crate in the alley directly opposite the stage depot. Well-hidden, he followed the stranger's movements, and the stranger didn't disappoint him. Moments after Munro entered the depot office, the man in the natty brown suit was positioning himself by its open side window.

As pre-arranged, Munro snapped his fingers. That was Dade Wakely's cue. He at once abandoned his perusal of a manifest and quit his desk to confront the burly Scot. Wakely was of stocky build and bespectacled; he had been in the transportation business his whole working life but, like Munro, was willing to try his hand at play-acting, if only this one time.

"Is this about the N and C Railroad payroll, Angus?" he asked.

"Right, Dade, and it can be delayed no longer," muttered Munro. "Those toilers laying track down south for the spur line haven't been paid in two months. They're threatening to down tools, so the Northern and Central have to take a chance."

The conversation continued. They lowered their voices, but not exactly to a whisper.

"Angus, *please* tell me there'll be an escort party. I mean — so big a cash shipment!"

"Close enough to thirty thousand, Dade. It'll be on the southbound leaving here day after tomorrow. Look, I'm as sorry as the sheriff, but . . . "

"*No* armed escort?"

"We can't recruit enough men, Dade. There just aren't enough heroes in Gould City. With the Duval gang still riding free, they fear the coach'll be ambushed and — they're mostly family men with no gizzard for a run-in with bandits. And you can hardly blame 'em."

"Hell, Angus, the crew, the passengers . . . !"

"They'll just have to take their chances. Sorry it has to be this way, Dade. Look, can we not be optimistic? While that coach is headed south, Duval and his men could be marauding across the border in Wyoming or hitting a bank in North-east Colorado."

Having said that, Munro cocked an ear, and not a moment too soon; he and Wakely were running out of lines and might not be as convincing if forced to ad-lib. He held a finger to his lips as he sidled to the side window. A full thirty seconds he waited before poking his head out. He withdrew and said, "Nobody out there."

"Not now," nodded the depot-boss. "But there was."

"It's to be hoped you're right," frowned Munro. "Had a feeling, did you?"

"It's instinct," declared Wakely. "My short hairs tingle when I suspect I'm being overheard. I can always tell. It's happened before."

"More power to your short hairs, Dade my friend," said Munro. "You'll have a word with Pete Reisner, will you not?"

"Pete'll be told," Wakely promised. "And you know you can count on him."

Munro moved to the street doorway, but did not show himself. Too soon, he decided. Turning, he remarked to Wakely, "Reisner's driven for this line a good long time. That's reason enough for him to hate road agents I'm sure but, for the Duval gang, he has a special antagonism. Could it be you know the reason? I don't ask you to betray a confidence, but . . . "

"I can tell you why he volunteered to drive the decoy coach," offered Wakely. "He's not much of a talker. On the other hand, he didn't swear me to secrecy or anything like that. It's simple, Angus. When Duval and his guns robbed a bank at Hadensworth five months back, an unarmed citizen was cut down — Pete's brother. Every run he's worked since that time, he's been *hoping* he'll drive into an ambush."

"Well, well, well," Munro nodded thoughtfully. "It would seem, day after tomorrow, I couldn't be sharing the seat with a better man."

He waited until he heard a clatter of hoofbeats, a horse being hard-ridden, before quitting the stage depot. As he started back to the sheriff's office, his young colleague came hustling across the street to fall in beside him.

"We got results," Mike? he asked.

"Mister Brown Suit took the bait," Mike said with relish.

"I had my eyes on him. For most of the time you were with Dade Wakely, he was snoopin' by the side window. Then he hurried to Alcott's Barn and, a couple of minutes later, he rode out southbound. Well, for two blocks. Then he turned into Kimler Street, which means he's headed west now."

"Phin will be pleased," grinned Munro.

Phin Judd took the news while swigging coffee brewed by the jailer.

"It's going well," he opined.

"Sounds like you're all set," remarked Greeber. "Gonna be the first time Duval gets more'n he bargained for."

"Makes better sense than mounting expeditions," declared Judd. "Dozen or more men getting saddlesores, searching all over the Dakotas for a robbers' roost and getting nowhere.

This might be the way, boys. This could do it."

★ ★ ★

The Texans and Enoch had noon-camped in a grove a short distance north of the stage route. It was a full ten minutes after they had kicked dirt onto their cook-fire and were about to pack their gear and saddle up again when they heard a horseman approaching from the east. Perfect timing, however unintentionally; had they smothered their fire a few minutes later, the rider might have glimpsed smoke-wisps above the trees.

"Some hombre's in one helluva hurry," Stretch commented.

Larry broke out his field glasses. True, they weren't far from the trail, but he was suddenly curious, feeling an urge to closely appraise the first rider to pass them since their departure from the Black Hills.

They hunkered, concealed at the

140

south edge of the grove. The horseman was coming into view and keeping his mount to a stiff pace. Stretch and Enoch followed his progress with interest, Larry even more so with the aid of his binoculars.

"Rigged like a city man," observed Enoch. "All in brown."

"What's his big hurry?" mused Larry. "He travels light, and that could mean . . . "

"He don't plan on bein' on this trail three or four more days," nodded Stretch. "Do I get to read your mind, runt?"

"Try," invited Larry.

The rider passed their vantage point and moved on westward still at speed; Larry didn't lower his glasses.

"You're wonderin' if there's a town not too far east and maybe big enough to have banks and a stage depot," guessed Stretch. "If that's where that fast rider's been, maybe he's a scout headed for wherever Duval's waitin'."

"Which could be Limbo Gulch,"

muttered Larry, while Enoch blinked at him. He passed the binoculars to Stretch. "We'll wait for you somewheres east. No wind today, so I figure I can backtrack him. You stay after that jasper. Mind now, you don't have to tag him all the way to the Gulch. All I want to be sure of is that's where he's headed.

"You said . . . " Enoch began a protest, but Stretch cut in on him.

"Changed your mind?" he challenged.

"Time enough later to explain why," nodded Larry.

"Whatever you say," shrugged Stretch. "I can wait."

They returned to the centre of the grove. First to saddle up and mount, the taller Texan made for the stage trail to dog the westbound rider. When Larry and Enoch broke cover, they rode eastward onto the trail, Larry intently studying ground, committing to memory the hoofprints of the brown-clad man's roan. He was concentrating and Enoch knew it, but curiosity plagued him.

"I have to stay quiet," he supposed. "Or — is it all right if I ask you something?"

"You can talk," said Larry, still reading sign. "I'll tell you when to button your lip."

"I'm remembering what Marshal Purl told us about Limbo Gulch," Enoch said hesitantly. "And how you — well — when we left there, it seemed no place for Blanco Jack to hole up, enough miners there to wipe out the whole gang."

"Back then, that's how everything seemed," nodded Larry. "Happens that way sometimes. You wouldn't savvy because, as if I have to remind you, you're young and green and Stretch and me, we've been tanglin' with owlhoots for longer'n you've lived."

"You sure *don't* have to remind me," sighed Enoch.

"I didn't get to thinkin' about it till long after we quit the Gulch," said Larry. "What it gets down to is this.

Mostly, what you see and what you're told is the way things are. You don't doubt it — till later, when you get to thinkin' on it."

"Can I ask what started you wondering?" frowned Enoch.

"Stretch told us what he learned in the saloon, chewin' the fat with a few miners," muttered Larry. "Didn't seem important at the time. The gulch is a mine camp. No women there 'cept the fat woman and the whores. Every hombre's single and them that's in business there, them that run the livery and the carpenter shop, they live by 'emselves."

"But it mightn't be that way?" prodded Enoch.

"Mightn't," said Larry. "For instance, I saw a feller totin' supper into Morcombe's place — two suppers. I just supposed him and Morcombe were gonna eat together, but maybe I was wrong, maybe the other supper was for Duval."

Enoch started convulsively.

144

"Holy Moses!"

"Don't fall off your horse," chided Larry. "I got no patience for greenhorns that fall off their horses."

"You're turning everything around!" complained Enoch. "The whole gang — using Limbo Gulch for their hideout? How could that be?"

"Look, kid, I'll say somethin' I say a lot." Larry was still backtracking the westbound rider, but nudging his mount to a trot. "I can be wrong. Nobody's smart all the time. I've been wrong before and I'll be wrong again — but maybe I'm right about Limbo Gulch." He forced himself to patience, stressing one point at a time. "Every shovel-stiff in that place don't have to be a Duval man. They're miners sure enough and they ain't drillin' and diggin' for nothin'. They're minin' gold. But Duval and his gunhands could be there and they all know it and they cover for him — Purl, the fat woman, the whole camp."

"Why would they . . . ?"

"My hunch is they've made a deal. For as long as Duval's bunch keep their paws off the gold cached there, they can hole up and the miners'll cover for 'em. Duval's the only one could be recognized anyway. When a posse stops by, them bandidos're rigged like miners and toilin' in the shafts. Duval just stays out of sight. He could hide in Morcombe's place or maybe a tunnel. And, as well as never tryin' to steal some miner's stash, maybe they pay 'em a cut from every job they pull."

"So the marshal's in cahoots with 'em too?"

"He'd have to be."

"By golly! No wonder Duval's so hard to find! The Gulch is just right for him, the perfect hideout!"

"If I'm right," said Larry.

"I'll bet you're right," enthused Enoch.

"Well," shrugged Larry. "I'll feel surer if Stretch tags that lone rider far enough to know he's headed for the Gulch."

The shadows of late afternoon were lengthening, but there was still no wind to erase the lone rider's tracks when they reached the point at which their route cut away from a trail extending north and south, obviously another stage trail. Larry had plenty to be thankful for. Visibility was good. He was able, after reading the sign that showed Gould City to be north and Moberley to the south and many more miles distant, to assure himself the rider had come from the north.

"Gould City," Enoch assumed.

"Probably," said Larry. He was scanning their surroundings for a camping place. "But we don't head there till Stretch gets back to us."

Some twenty-five yards from the turn-off, a semi-circle of boulders would break the force of any wind blowing up during the night. They gathered firewood. Larry set about making a fire, leaving Enoch to tend the horses and, guessing it would be some time before his partner rejoined them, prepared supper for two.

After sundown, the temperature dropped and, studying the sky, Larry noted the movement of clouds; there would be little moonlight, if any. He slept until 10 p.m. with the youth sitting guard, then rose draped in his blanket and took over from him.

Enoch was in deep slumber when, in the wee small hours, guided by the fireglow, the taller Texan returned. Larry at once threw more wood on the fire and set the skillet and coffee-pot in position.

"Won't take long to heat up," he muttered, as Stretch yawned and dismounted. "Squat and warm your bones, beanpole. I'll take care of your horse."

"Hope we ain't movin' on till mornin'," drawled Stretch. "That strawberry roan's some strong critter, got speed too, but I ran him hard. He's earned his rest."

Larry tended the roan, secured it with the other animals and came back to the fire. While waiting for his overdue supper with his belly growling, Stretch assured him that, once again, one of his hunches had paid off.

"He's in Limbo Gulch now," frowned Larry.

"Has to be," declared Stretch. "I made damn sure. And you can bet I made sure nobody spotted me, includin' any lookout atop the near wall of the Gulch. So . . . " He stifled another yarn. "Not all them hombres're regular prospectors, huh?"

"It could explain why no posse could find Duval's hideout," said Larry. "It just don't *look* like a hideout. A search party believes what it sees." He repeated the suspicions he had confided to Enoch. Stretch emptied the contents of the skillet onto his plate, satisfied his ravenous appetite and listened with keen interest. Having said it all, Larry concluded, "Next place we head for's Gould City to the north, because the scout could've been there — likely was. Signpost tells me we could make it before noon, if we get started early."

"We'll have to parley with the law," warned Stretch, still plying his fork. "We ready for that?"

"Ask me again when we get there," said Larry. "We know from Dex Beech that the Pegrum sheriff's a Texas-hater from way back. In Gould City, I aim to find out what kind of badge-toters we have to deal with 'fore I brace 'em."

With his plate near cleared, Stretch scathingly opined, "No badge-toter could be as crooked a skunk as that Limbo Gulch marshal."

"Ain't that the truth," scowled Larry.

"He's fed that mess of bull to every searcher ever stopped by," guessed Stretch. "Duval's gang wouldn't dare show up there. And, all the time, Duval sits pat and his gunhawks pass 'emselves off as miners and who could tell the difference? Sweet set-up. They all know, the prospectors, Purl, the bunch at Goldie's Place, all the women."

"Safe guess why the rider you followed

was hightailin' it to the Gulch," said Larry. "He learned somethin', maybe in Gould City. Could be mucho dinero leavin' that town soon, strong-box full of cash on a north or southbound coach."

"And the only way we'll find out . . ." began Stretch.

"Right," nodded Larry. "Like it or not, we powwow with the local law." When Stretch finished his coffee, he urged him, "Catch your sleep."

"Wasn't about to volunteer to sit guard," Stretch wearily assured him. "I'm bone-tired."

They cooked and ate breakfast after sun-up. Supplies were getting low. Whatever else they did at Gould City, they would need to provision up again.

While they followed the trail leading to Gould City, the taller drifter asked what seemed a fair question.

"*How* do we check on the local law?"

"We ask somebody," decided Larry.

"Well, not just anybody. Better we parley with some important citizen, a responsible jasper like, for instance, a banker, a councilman, maybe the Western Union man."

"I've never been all that leery of lawmen," remarked Enoch. "But I guess you always had to be."

"Damn right," declared Stretch.

"All kinds get paid to keep the peace," said Larry. "We've run into plenty fair-square badge-toters — and plenty we wouldn't trust no farther'n we could throw a bull-buffalo."

"And plenty that can't abide us and our ways," muttered Stretch. "Always bellyachin', always claimin' we — how do they say it, runt?"

"Take the law into our own hands," grouched Larry.

"Isn't that what you do anyway?" Enoch couldn't suppress a grin.

"That ain't what *we* call it," retorted Larry.

"So what do you call it?" prodded Enoch.

"We get things done," shrugged Stretch. "Right?"

"Yeah, that's it," agreed Larry.

They did reach the quite impressive seat of Gould County before noon. It was a little after 11.10 a.m. when they idled their mounts into the broad and busy main street, Larry warily appraising locals on the sidewalks.

Two blocks from the south edge of town, the trouble-shooters appraised a pedestrian crossing ahead of them. He was typical of every frontier medico they had known, they decided, slight of build, no youngster, spectacles, placid expression, grey hair, derby, black jacket and grey pants. And he carried a small black valise. Watching him reach the west sidewalk and stroll uptown, they pegged him for the man they needed. The little valise was the clincher, and who better than a local doctor to inform them of the temper of the local law? Doctors, they had found, considered themselves neutrals, never bothering themselves with the wrangling of cattle town administration.

They nudged their mounts onward, keeping the elderly man in view and, soon, were passing the sheriff's office. It happened that the younger deputy was watching from the street doorway. Until this moment, he had an ear cocked to the worried conversation of Angus Munro and the sheriff. Now, staring after the tall riders, he mouthed an oath and whirled to glare at the elder lawmen, who eyed him with raised brows.

"You're fazed, laddie," Munro observed.

"Something wrong, Mike?" asked Judd.

"Who does he think he's foolin'?" fumed Mike.

"Who?" demanded inquisitive Saul Greeber.

"Des he think that damn beard could fool *me*?" scowled Mike. "Different clothes, ridin' a dapple instead of his sorrel — and the whiskers? No chance! I'd know him anywhere! If he lost an eye, his hair and his teeth and if his nose was broken, I'd *still* peg him!"

"Now that you got us curious as all git-out, suppose you tell us who in tarnation you're gripin' about?" challenged Greeber.

"My cousin — second cousin twice removed — or whatever he is — him with his big reputation." Mike was still scowling. "It's a distant relationship, but we got the same family name."

"Hell's sakes, Saul," breathed Judd. "He's talking about Larry Valentine."

"Tricked out like a tinhorn, him and his partner," Mike said bitterly. "Tryin' to disguise 'emselves."

"Och, it's a mean laddie bears a grudge against his own kinsman," sighed Munro.

"I don't think Mike's really toting a grudge," Judd said with a knowing grin. "He's just a little jealous of his record. Come on, Mike, the truth."

"What lawman wouldn't be jealous?" grouched Mike.

"There's a more important question

for consideration here," reflected Munro. "That question being what brings those trouble-shooters to Gould City?"

"I'd like an answer to that one," decided Judd.

The three riders moved their mounts close to the sidewalk and addressed the man they had followed. He paused to accord them a bland smile.

"Got somethin' to ask you, Doc," said Larry.

"Won't take up too much of your time, Doc," drawled Stretch. "We figure we can rely on you for a straight answer."

"Is this county satisfied with its lawmen, or are some honest citizens leery of 'em?" enquired Larry. "And another thing. You happen to know if they turn hostile when a Texan fronts up to 'em?"

His questions drew a question.

"Are you gentlemen or your young friend in need of medical attention?"

"No, we're good and healthy," frowned Larry.

"That's fortunate, because I'm no doctor," was the amused rejoinder. "Lucas is the name, Martin Lucas, attorney at law. As a matter of fact, I'm county attorney here." He chuckled — Stretch's confusion was comical — and patted his bag. "This contains a few documents, but no medicines, no surgical instruments. I suppose it does resemble the kind of valises favored by our resident medicos, so you can be excused for your error."

"No offense, Mister Lucas," muttered Stretch.

"Apologies unnecessary," Lucas assured them. "As for your questions, I'm delighted to describe Sheriff Phineas Judd and his aides as fine officers with no black mark on their record, not even a vague hint of corruption nor partisan attitudes. And it's unlikely they'd have any animosity toward Texans, since Phin's younger deputy is himself Texas born."

"Gracias," acknowledged Larry. "And I got to say it, Mister Lucas. You look a lot more like a doc than a lawyer."

"Well, as the local doctors are fine fellows and good friends of mine, I think I'll take that as a compliment," grinned Lucas. He gestured downtown. "Sheriff's office is that way, other side of the street."

After the newcomers wheeled their mounts and pointed them downtown, Stretch remarked to Enoch, "Now maybe you'll believe what Larry tells you about us. We ain't perfect. We can make mistakes."

"I guess you and Larry're happy the sheriff's got a Texan for a deputy," said Enoch.

"I don't care where Judd's deputies got born," said Larry. "We know they're on the square, and that's what important."

Mike was again watching from the law office doorway.

"Comin' back now," he reported over his shoulder. "Look like they're headed right for here."

"So we're gonna see a reunion,"

said Judd. "You and your notorious kinsman."

"Reunion? We've never even met." Mike turned and advanced to his boss's desk. "But it's him sure enough. Think of all the bulletins I've read, the newspaper pictures I've seen."

"See here now," Judd said gently. "You're related like it or not and he and his partner aren't the subjects of outstanding warrants, so why don't we keep it friendly? Let's just listen to them."

Over by the cell-block doorway, Saul Greeber filled and lit his corncob and waited with keen interest. They heard the three horses out front. The visitors were dismounting and looping their reins. Now, with Larry leading, they climbed to the law office porch and entered. Larry guessed the seated Judd to be senior lawman herein. Ignoring the younger deputy's intent stare, he began talking.

"Sheriff Judd, this young feller's just called 'Kid'. I'm Waco Webb.

My partner's Brazos Billy Terhune and . . . "

"You're a damn liar, Larry Valentine!" accused Mike.

Larry looked him over — coldly.

"Be thankful you got an arm in a sling," he growled.

"Be *mighty* thankful, sonny," Stretch advised. "That busted wing's savin' your front teeth. My 'ol buddy gets powerful mean when you call him a liar."

"Mike has a right — Emerson," countered Judd, and two bearded jaws sagged. "He knows who you are, and he certainly knows your partner Valentine, because he's a Valentine, a cousin three times removed or some such."

Larry grimaced, nudged his Stetson off his brow and traded stares with Deputy Mike Valentine.

"Kin — me and you?" he challenged. "But, damn it, you're a whole lot younger, there's too many years 'tween us."

"What's that got to do with

anything?" retorted Mike. "Your father had brothers and cousins. You'd have distant relatives all over Texas, all over the country."

Munro puffed at his meeschaum and nodded approvingly.

"Great breeders, the Texans."

"How about this?" Larry appealed to his partner.

"I likely got as many kinfolks scattered," shrugged Stretch. "No way we could guess you'd run into this buck, runt." He did not sound a hundred percent in favor as he added, "A Valentine with a tin star."

"Could we get down to business?" suggested Judd. "This isn't the first time a visitor lied to me about his identity. I don't resent it. When the Lone Star tearaways start using alias, I figure they have a good reason."

"Yeah, well, *I* resent . . . " began Mike.

"We need cool heads here if anything important's to be said," insisted Munro.

"What we're here for's plenty

important," declared Larry. "For starters . . . " He eyed his distant relative again, "can you lock that street-door onehanded?"

"Do it, Mike," urged Judd. "Strick secrecy, Valentine?"

"Damn right," said Larry. "Next question. You got a newspaper here?"

"The *Gould County Chronicle*," nodded Judd. "Oliver Aiken, editor and founder."

"And he's got a nose for news," drawled Greeber.

"So Oliver Aiken, editor and founder, gets told nothin', okay?" challenged Larry.

"You never heard of freedom of the press?" Judd asked mildly.

"I hear about it all the time and sometimes it's useful," said Larry. "But not *this* time."

"The scribbler can learn about it later maybe," offered Stretch. "When it's all over."

"I'll go along with that," decided Judd. "Sit, if you can find enough seats here. Let's observe the courtesies, gents. You know Deputy Mike Valentine. I'm Phineas Judd, mostly called Phin. Meet my other deputy, Angus Munro, and our county jailer Saul Greeber."

Mike secured the door. Smokes were lit; they made themselves as comfortable as possible, after which Larry warned he would have to begin with another question.

"And don't jump when I ask," he muttered. "You know our style, so you know we're never in cahoots with bandidos. We're for the law."

"In your own rough way," complained Mike.

"Rough," agreed Judd.

"But effective," grinned Munro.

"So what do you have to ask of us, Valentine?" demanded Judd.

"Tomorrow or the day after, real soon anyway," prodded Larry, "Is there gonna be big dinero shipped out of Gould City — on a stage maybe?"

The sheriff and his staff weren't ready for that. They had no hope of masking their reaction; stunned glances passed back and forth. Greeber swore explosively. Judd, first to recover his composure, became wary.

"I'll consider my answer to that question," he told Larry. "After — and you'll have to agree this is fair — you give your reason for asking it."

"I call that fair enough, runt," said Stretch. "We can talk to 'em. The lawyer trusts 'em. So that ought to be good enough for us."

"Howzat again?" frowned Greeber.

"Lawyer?" asked Munro.

"Name of Martin Lucas," said Larry. "We mistook him for a doc. Well, hell, we were never here before, had to be sure we could trust you 'fore we laid all this on you."

Judd was taken aback, but in a good-humored way.

"You felt obliged to have Marty Lucas vouch for us?"

"We've been called reckless," said Larry. "Don't believe it."

"Ain't true," said Stretch. "We stay

careful, we stay alive — and out of reach of ornery badgetoters."

"Prudence is a virtue," Munro said poker-faced.

"All right, you satisfied yourselves as to our integrity," said Judd. "Now tell me why you asked about consignments of cash moving out of Gould County."

"I've figured out where Blanco Duval and his gang hole up," Larry announced. "But that's only the half of it. On our way here, we spotted a rider headed for the Black Hills."

"Made damn sure *he* didn't spot *us*," interjected Stretch.

"And, for our money, he's a Duval spy and he learned somethin' here," offered Larry. "Any Duval man could scout any town. You know that for a fact, because yeller-haired Duval himself's the only one you could hope to spot. The rest of 'em hide their faces behind bandannas or use hoods."

Mike Valentine stared incredulously at his kinsman, shook his head and muttered, "I don't know why I'm surprised. It's their crazy luck?"

"Sonofagun," breathed Greeber.

"Describe the rider you suspect of being a Duval scout," frowned Judd.

"Brown town duds, derby to match," drawled Stretch.

Judd sighed resignedly and checked his watch.

"We're in for a long conference," he predicted. "Saul, fix coffee. Angus, go to the Belden Cafe, arrange delivery of some food. Like it or not, *we're* in cahoots with these trouble-shooters."

6

Combined Operation

FURTHER conversation was postponed until Munro and a waitress from the cafe carried laden trays into Judd's office. When the girl departed, Mike re-secured the street-door. Plates were distributed along with forks, and Greeber set two coffeepots on the stove. Judd broke out a bottle and set it aside. The conspirators stopped smoking and began eating. And Enoch was in awe.

He forked up food, munched and thought back over the events following his quitting his hometown and encountering the famous adventurers. So much had happened since then. Small wonder his elders of Maddenville scoffed at his ambition to collect the price on Blanco Jack's head. This was all a new experience for him, new, exciting, intimidating too. Throw in his ten cents worth of comment when all these professionals got to talking? Not likely. By golly, no. Larry would probably paddle his backside.

While eating, Judd assured the Texans he and his men had been well aware of the man in the brown suit. It had to be the same man they had sighted westbound.

"We obliged him, you might say," grinned Munro.

"Guessed what he was here for," said Judd. "So Angus and Wakely, the depot manager, played a little scene for him."

"I was watchin' from the alley opposite," offered Mike. "He grabbed the bait, count on that. He was listenin' at a window."

The trouble-shooters were impressed to the point of congratulating Judd and his aides on their chicanery.

"Thank you," Judd said dryly. "It was sly and underhand, a cunning trick, so it's natural you'd approve."

"I'm guessin' right I reckon," grinned Larry. "Decoy coach, no cash aboard, just sharpshooters."

"We'll talk of that presently," countered Judd. "I'm waiting to hear why you're so sure you found Duval's hideout."

"Limbo Gulch it's called," said Larry. "Mine camp in the Black Hills."

"Limbo Gulch and every other camp in those hills, every claim, has been searched by posses," protested Mike.

"Keep talkin', hot shot," urged Greeber.

The incident at Limbo Gulch was recounted in detail, the attitude of Ezra Purl and the miners, any of whom could be Duval men in disguise, the shooting at the saloon, Enoch's exchange of shots with a would-be horse-thief, then the leave-taking and the resumption of their journey east, the sighting and backtracking of the brown-suited scout.

"And Emerson made sure the spy ended up in Limbo Gulch," mused Judd.

"*Dead* sure," nodded Stretch.

"It all makes sense," Judd agreed. He had finished eating. He took a sip of coffee, rose and moved to the large map tacked to the wall right off the cell-block entrance, and now the trouble-shooters noted a wide area had been circled in pencil. Judd took up a pencil and made a mark. "Here, approximately anyway, is Limbo Gulch. Centre of the circle. They've made raids all over this region and, by killing their tracks and always returning to the same base, have dodged every pursuit party hunting them."

"From the heights above the Gulch . . . " began Munro.

"Yes, Angus," said Judd. "Lookouts. Duval has ample warning of an approaching posse. Where does he hide? Anybody's guess. As Valentine says, a hundred and one holes for him at the Gulch. The dead end of a mine shaft could be camouflaged for instance, a compartment beyond. He escapes detection simply by staying quiet until told the searchers have left."

"And everybody at Limbo Gulch keeps his mouth shut," Mike said grimly.

"Two incentives I'd think," said Munro. "One, they're paid a little something for their silence. Two, they can't find the courage to tip Duval's hand — they fear reprisal."

Judd came back to his desk and uncorked a bottle to spike coffee cups. He put his eyes on the youngest party present. "What age are you, boy?"

"Sixteen, sir," said Enoch.

Munro shook his head sadly. Judd grimaced.

"To protect yourself, you had to kill a man. How do you feel about that?"

"Well, I try," shrugged Enoch. "I mean I try to think like Larry and Stretch. It was something I had to do. Had to fire, didn't I? That thief didn't draw his six-gun just to spook me. He fired first and his bullet came awful close. I don't feel good — but I'm not ashamed either."

"Satisfactory answer, Phin?" asked Munro.

"It'll do," said Judd.

"I answered all your questions, sheriff . . . " Larry began impatiently.

"There's one I didn't think to ask till now," interrupted Judd. "What made you and Emerson decide to hunt Duval in the first place?"

"Tell him, runt," urged Stretch. "No reason he oughtn't know about Dex Beech's grief."

Larry kept it brief. The sheriff and his aides showed no surprise upon being told the drifters were behind bars when approached by the Diamond B boss. They listened to a repetition of the rancher's account of the raid led by Duval, the gunning down of the Beech brothers and the subsequent demise of the grief-stricken Madeline. By the end of it, Larry's distant relative was slightly more cordial.

"That'd be reason enough for you to risk your neck," he remarked. "You and your partner both."

"Good enough reason, sure," nodded Larry.

"And we . . . " began Stretch.

"Had nothin' better to do anyway," guessed Mike.

Stretch frowned at him.

"How'd you know I was gonna say that?"

"It just seemed like somethin' you'd say," said Mike, and he managed a grin for the first time since their arrival.

The meal ended. The Texans accepted short shots of good rye and Larry eyed Judd expectantly.

"Decoy coach?" he prodded. "C'mon, you can tell us."

"Don't forget we're on your side," said Stretch.

Judd was suddenly uncomfortable. Munro contributed another sigh and added one of his sad head-shakes. Mike grimaced impatiently and Greeber winced.

"What's the matter here?" demanded Larry.

"We've planned so carefully," complained Judd. "Arranged for the coach and the best driver we could hope for. Made certain preparations . . . "

"We were all set," muttered Munro.

"Then — two big disappointments," said Judd. "One last night, the other this morning. Two very willing volunteers, mighty reliable men and both sure shots, but they've had to pull out, just can't come along."

"The original plan," explained Munro, "was for Phin, Mike and two volunteers to travel inside the coach — with a better than adequate armory — and me playing shot-gun guard up top with Pete Reisner, the driver."

"Six of us," said Judd. "Even if Duval's whole gang ambushed us — as expected — we'd have had the element of surprise on our side."

"Sounds good," shrugged Stretch.

"Smart strategy," approved Larry. "We've pulled that trick a time or two, and it works fine."

"Last night, one of our volunteers had to call in Doc Shields," said Judd. "Colic. Bad case. He'll be laid up three more days at least, Doc says, and we planned on leaving eight o'clock tomorrow morning. About four hours ago, the other man had to pull out. I don't blame him. His wife gave him the happy news over breakfast."

"Said she was keepin' it a secret from him," Mike said in disgust. "You want to guess the happy news? She's gonna make a daddy of him."

"Well, he's jumping for joy, all caught up in fatherhood fever," grouched Judd. "Wouldn't think of making the decoy run with us, too much worry for his wife, bad for her in her condition."

"And this'un ain't helped none," Greeber jeered at Mike. "Bustin' his doggone arm — and it had to be his gunarm."

The trouble-shooters eyed each other, grinning in grim anticipation.

"What're you frettin' about?" Larry

challenged Judd. "We can still do it. No way you can leave *us* out of it."

"Including me," Enoch quickly offered.

"Forget it, kid," growled Larry.

"Hey, I've come this far," protested Enoch. "You can't cut me loose now!"

"Got to," Larry said firmly. "Be reasonable. You're willin' enough, but sixteen is too young for this kind of action."

"Far too young," declared Judd. "I couldn't permit it, young feller." He studied the Texans, his hopes rising. "So you're volunteering?"

"Try and stop 'em," scowled Mike.

"Wipe that hostile look off your kisser, cousin," chided Larry. "*I* didn't break your arm. Sheriff, the kid's out of it, he stays here. And you and my partner'll move easier if there's only the two of you inside the coach. Four with extra guns'd be too tight-packed. With Stretch shootin' from one side, you shootin' from the other, you'll . . . "

"Remember the old days?" Greeber

dryly remarked to Munro. "When Phin used to be in charge here?"

"We'll let Valentine finish," suggested Judd. "After all, he and Emerson — uh — have had some experience."

"My spot'll be the roof," Larry continued. "Maybe you planned on stashing a couple trunks up there, some baggage to make it look like a regular passenger run, but there won't be room enough now. All I need is a tarp. I'll be hid under it till the ambushers make their play." He glanced at Munro. "You'll be on the seat with the driver. Too bad about that. Shot-gun guard's always wide open, apt to be the first target they cut loose at. Well, I'll cover you and the driver as best I can."

"That's it, huh?" frowned Judd.

"Well, you're the boss, but it sounds fine to me," said Larry.

"Phin it's close enough to your plan anyway," said Munro.

"Sure," agreed Judd. "Five instead of the original seven. Emerson and

I inside with plenty of elbow room, Valentine on the roof . . . ."

"Too bad you and the driver'll be sittin' shots," Stretch said to Munro.

"Unless they aim for our heads, Phil Reisner and myself'll be giving a good account of ourselves," smiled the Scot.

"Since everything seems settled, and taking it for granted the young feller'll seal his lips, they might as well see our extra precautions," said Judd.

"Don't worry about the kid," said Larry. "We'll check into a hotel, and that's where he'll stay."

"Till it's over," stressed Stretch, eyeing the youth sternly. "You hear what we're tellin' you, boy?"

"I hear," sighed Enoch.

"And he'll say nothin' he's heard said here," Larry assured Judd. "Now what was that about — extra . . . ?"

"Precautions," Judd nodded to Greeber, who unlocked the jailhouse entrance. "Curly Tebbut's idea. He built these jackets in secret. Well, not exactly jackets. More like vests."

"Saul couldn't carry them out of there by himself," said Munro, and he rose and followed Greeber into the jail.

"They're heavy, but not so heavy Angus and Reisner can't wear them," Judd told the Texans. "Tebbut experimented, kind of, with different thicknesses of steel plate. They've been tried on and tested, so we know they'll block bullets."

When Munro and the jailer brought the shields to light, the drifters first assumed them to be regular vests. They were painted dull blue; there were straps in front for fastening them to the wearer. But then they were placed on the floor and did not crumple like vests of cloth; Munro and Greeber set them down with a metallic thud.

"Holy sufferin' Hannah!" breathed Stretch.

"Can you move in them contraptions?" frowned Larry.

"I'll show you," offered Munro. He

lifted the larger one, thrusting his hands through the armholes, straightened up and began securing the buckles. "Notice the dents? We took 'em out of town to test 'em. Those dents were made by forty-four slugs, close-range and long-range."

"If Angus or Reisner are hit, they'll take quite a jolt, but bullets won't penetrate," explained Judd. "And they'll have freedom of movement. Reisner's sure he can handle his team. If it goes like a regular hold-up, Angus'll throw down an empty shot-gun and the empty strongbox."

"And that'll be the signal," said Munro, rising to his full height, displaying his protection. "We'll have loaded weapons concealed. When the strong-box hits the ground . . . "

"We attack," Judd said bluntly. "Emerson and I open up from inside the coach, Angus and Reisner cut loose and you, Valentine, will probably down two or more from the roof. This time, whatever trap Duval sets is gonna backfire on him."

"You like this, runt?" grinned Stretch.

"You know it," growled Larry.

"Wow!" was Enoch's reaction.

"You won't be there to see it," muttered Mike. "That don't bother me none — but I hate *me* not bein' there."

"Don't start the same old speech," Greeber chided him. "Left-handed, you're no use with a pistol, so that's that."

Munro took a few clumping steps back and forth. Greeber passed him a Winchester from the rack and he demonstrated the ease and alacrity with which he could cock it.

"I'd not attempt to run the length of Main Street wearing this armor," he remarked. "But I'm convinced, and Pete Reisner agrees, it'll serve the purpose it's designed for."

"I can see you heroes are impressed," said Judd.

"Seems like we're all set," enthused Larry. "Where do we board?"

"Alley behind the depot, eight o'clock," said Judd.

"We all get to down a good breakfast 'fore we start out," approved Stretch.

Mike stared at him, then at Larry, and asked, "Is he always hungry? Hell, we just finished lunch."

"Next to fightin', eatin's what he does best," said Larry. "Speakin' of eatin', you want to have supper with us tonight?"

"Why don't you do that, Mike?" urged the sheriff. "You said you're jealous of his reputation, but that's no reason you can't be a friendly relative."

"Anybody gonna name us a good hotel?" demanded Larry.

"Good dinin' room at the Palace," offered Greeber. "It's a real clean place, got bathrooms and snug beds, plumb respectable too." He grinned and added, "Respectable place though it is, they mightn't turn you away."

"You call me Larry," offered Larry. "He's Stretch, he's Kid. Supper. What d'you say?"

"Well, all right," nodded Mike. "Thanks for the invite and — I'll quit bellyachin' about my arm and try and be a little more sociable."

"Triple J Livery for your horses," Judd advised as Enoch and the trouble-shooters rose to leave. "Half-block uptown from the hotel. So — until tomorrow morning?"

"Back of the stage depot, eight o'clock," promised Larry. "We'll be there."

Mike followed them out to the porch to direct them to the hotel and stable. They headed first for the Triple J, leading their animals. Now, out of earshot of the local lawmen, Enoch gave vent to his disappointment and disgust.

"Me stuck in a hotel room. Damn! I didn't want it to be this way. All along, I've been counting on getting in on the action, being there for the showdown."

"Kid, we made you no guarantees," Larry reminded him. "If it was some other set-up, us findin' the Duval bunch camped in a basin for instance, keepin' 'em pinned down, tradin' fire with 'em from good cover, we'd likely deal you in."

"But not this kind of a set-up," said Stretch. "Too chancy, boy. Lurin' 'em into a shootout, ridin' in a decoy coach, is somethin' else again."

"It'd be no more dangerous for me than for you," argued Enoch.

"Wrong," Stretch shook his head emphatically. "You made your first kill in Limbo Gulch, but that was one against one. This'll be different — and a whole lot wilder."

"It could go either way," muttered Larry. "They might block the trail, then again they could break cover in back of us and, if the driver gets riled up, he might just decide to give his team their heads. Duval and his guns'll chase us and it'll be a runnin' fight. We've been in that kind of action . . ."

"Oftener'n we can tally," recalled Stretch.

" . . . and we savvy how to get the job done," continued Larry, "how to protect ourselves too. But, with you along, we'd be frettin' about protectin' you."

"I'd be just a nuisance, is that what you mean?" grouched Enoch.

"That what you want to be?" challenged Larry.

Enoch shrugged defeatedly. "I guess not."

The stablehand at the Triple J Livery obviously picked up an extra dollar by steering new arrivals to a local gambling house. To him, the tall men looked to be well-heeled sporting men, so he made his pitch.

"If you gents're lookin' for high-stake game, Gault's Casino's the place for you. Rollo Gault runs an honest house."

"'Obliged," Larry acknowledged. "We'll keep him in mind."

"Stayin' long?"

"Couple days."

Larry paid the man and, having

unslung their gear, the three strangers made for the Palace Hotel. There, mindful the Fourth Estate was represented in this town, the Texans registered under their aliases. They asked for and were assigned a double for themselves and a single for their young companion on the second floor.

A disgruntled Enoch settled into the single while Larry and Stretch stowed their gear in the double, tested the beds and decided how they should spend the rest of this afternoon, hot baths, clean shirts, rest and talk, in that order. Returning to his room after his bath, Enoch flopped on his bed and mentally reviewed his recent adventures. Big change in his life, he reflected, since beginning his quest and falling in with the heroes of his childhood. Was he as clumsy now? It didn't seem so. He was, he assured himself, gaining confidence, feeling considerably older than when he had ridden out of Maddenville. Was he missing Maddenville? Well, sure. His hometown after all, and Imogene was there. And would he see Maddenville again? Well, of course. Sixteen is a zesty age. Filled with the optimism and not a little of the presumption of youth, it never occurred to him that he might face further perils with the tough Texans nor that, unlike them, he would not be a survivor.

Would Imogene believe he had been in a life or death situation, had killed to defend himself? She would be incredulous, he supposed, and others even more so. Her father for instance, Uncle Gus, Carl Engle, Deputy Harroway and certainly Sheriff Francis P. O'Gorman.

That was the extent of his reverie. He enjoyed the resilience of youth, but the days since his meeting the Texans had been the most exciting of his life, the nights broken by his taking a turn at guard duty. Came now the predictable delayed reaction; he sank into deep sleep and stayed that way till Larry rapped on his door to inform him they'd be descending to the dining-room in ten minutes.

Deputy Michael Valentine was awaiting them in the lobby, swapping remarks with the desk-clerk. He traded greetings with his notorious kinsman, his manner less antagonistic now. In the dining-room, the veterans, the lawman in his twenties and the youth chose a table and inspected the bill of fare.

"Great steaks here — melt in your mouth," offered Mike. "It'll have to be the chicken pie for me. I can manage it left-handed, but that's okay. They do elegant chicken pie."

They gave their order. Larry was then moved to remark, "You're used to this place, must've eaten here before."

"Just twice," said Mike, grinning blandly. "You hot shots are marriage-shy. I'm not. Her name's Wilma Ferris and I've been courtin' her near a year. You wouldn't know about courtin', Larry."

"No," Larry admitted.

"They like bein' taken to dinner,"

said Mike. "When a travellin' show comes to Gould, she likes that too."

"You and the little lady named the weddin' date?" asked Stretch.

"Not even betrothed yet," shrugged Mike. "I put a little in my bank account every payday, keep on courtin' her and hope for her to come round."

"My girl's name is Imogene," Enoch announced. "But she doesn't want to be my girl and her pa doesn't approve of me and I don't reckon she'll *ever* come round."

Larry grimaced in exasperation, Stretch grinned indulgently and Mike showed a little more interest in the kid from Wyoming. The waitress delivered their supper. As he began eating, Mike suggested to him, "If you don't reckon she'll ever come round, she mightn't be the girl for you anyway. Ever think of that?"

"No, but I should've," frowned Enoch. "Yeah, you got a point. And what's my rush? Got my whole life ahead of me, right?"

"Right," nodded Mike.

"Your Wilma ain't sure how she feels about things, Mike?" asked Larry.

"It's my job." Mike continued in a between-us-men way.

"You know how some women are. They fret about how it'd be, married to a lawman. Phin and Angus're bachelors and happy enough. Why they stayed single, that's their business and I don't pry. But I aim to get married and go right on bein' a lawman. All Wilma needs is time and persuasion, and I'm in no hurry."

"That's smart thinkin'," approved Stretch. "Never hustle a female."

Half-way through their first course, Mike matched stares with his kinsman and declared, "I was pretty much like you after I quit Texas and started travellin' round, might've ended up exactly like you."

"That a fact?" prodded Larry.

"I don't mean I kept gettin' into fights or tanglin' with outlaws," said Mike. "But I sure was restless. Kept driftin' all over till I came to Gould City and met Wilma. Same day I met her, a deputy turned in his badge. Seems he was city-born homesick for Milwaukee."

"So you tried for his job and got it," guessed Stretch.

"Made up your mind?" asked Larry. "Just like that?"

"A man ought to have steady work," said Mike.

"Give thanks you ain't as restless as us tumble-weeds," Larry said soberly.

"The idea of settlin' here — it felt right," said Mike. "Phin Judd is plenty wise and so's Angus. I got sworn in, but just temporarily. They put me on trial for a half-year, taught me things, kept an eye on me till I proved myself. Now I'm a regular deputy and I use my badge — not just my gun and my fists."

"Runt . . . " Stretch grinned wryly, "I think Cousin Mike's tryin' to tell us somethin'."

"Fine by me," said Larry. "Oughtn't

be anything a Valentine can't say to a Valentine."

"It's just this," offered Mike. "Since I got to be a deputy, there's been three times a booze-ornery troublemaker changed his mind about pullin' a gun on me — and saved his life. It was close quarters all three times and I wasn't about to let 'em blow a hole through me. I'd have beat their speed and, that close, could I risk aimin' for an arm or a leg? But I didn't have to draw, because none of them drew on me. And why? The badge, Larry. Some hard talk. And the badge."

Larry swallowed a well-masticated chunk of steak and assured a younger Valentine, "I respect you, because you got good ideas and a brain in your head. And you're right about the badge but, for your own sake, you got to remember somethin' else about it. That six-pointed star can cool *some* hotheads, no arguments about that. Trouble is — another kind of hothead's apt to use it for a target."

"Damn right," agreed Mike. "Phin's told me that. So has Angus."

"Well, you're workin' with smart badge-toters and they'll steer you right," said Larry.

"You won't appreciate what I'm gonna ask you now," predicted Mike.

"Ask anyway," Larry invited.

"You've put many a badman six feet under, you and Stretch," said Mike. "If you'd been wearin' badges, maybe they'd be in prison instead of some hell-town Boot Hill. I don't mean you're trigger-happy, Larry, but . . . "

"You got *that* correct," muttered Stretch. "Trigger-happy we ain't."

"Don't forget we've taken plenty alive," said Larry.

"That's so," Mike conceded.

"We try, Mike, you can believe that," declared Larry.

"They always get their chance. If they surrender peaceable — no shootin'. If they pull iron — we defend ourselves."

"And you can't lick your wander-itch." Mike sounded sympathetic now.

"So, everywhere you wander, it'll keep on happenin'."

They had finished their first course. While waiting for their dessert, Larry and his distant relative, by mutual agreement and to the relief of Stretch and Enoch, switched the talk to family. In vain, but with good humor, they tried to work out the intricacies of their blood-tie, recalling various uncles and aunts and other elders of the clan Valentine of Texas. They could have saved their breath; there were just too many Valentines. The meal ended on a congenial note, Mike leaving to visit his lady friend and her family, the drifters repairing to the second-floor gallery for their after-supper smokes and a disinterested appraisal of the main street, Enoch to take a stroll.

"One thing you ain't sorry about, runt," guessed Stretch. "Mike's busted wing."

"It's Judd's deal now," shrugged Larry. "He's the boss and he'd never take a man who can't handle a gun, any more'n I'd take along a green kid like Enoch. And you're right, I ain't sorry Mike has to stay behind." He squinted at the glowing end of his cigar. "Maybe he'll die in harness anyway. A lot of lawmen do. But I hope he wins his Wilma long before then, hope he gets to be a husband and sire a kid."

"There'll always be kill-crazy thieves, amigo, all kinds of owlhoot scum," Stretch said softly. "So there'll always have to be regular lawmen — and fools like us that know no better'n to fight outlaws like lawmen do."

"Not exactly like lawmen do," corrected Larry.

"No," grinned Stretch. "We got our own ways."

★ ★ ★

After breakfast next morning, the tall men repeated their orders and Enoch gave the impression he was resigned to having to wait out their return from the decoy run. From the hotel, the trouble-shooters toted their rifles to the east alley paralleling Main and strolled to the rear of the stage depot.

Gould City was coming alive, another day beginning, its citizens and the editor of the local paper unaware it would be a day to be remembered by a select group, the local lawmen, the manager of the stage depot, a hard-boiled veteran driver name of Reisner, two drifters and a youth with a craving to win a $5000 bounty.

There was little conversation when the Texans arrived. Blunt-featured, tobacco-chewing Peter Reisner was already in position, a poncho covering his bulletproof vest. Angus Munro, wearing the same kind of protection, made slow work of climbing up beside him. Judd was already seated inside, packing a belted colt and nursing a sawn-off shot-gun. Larry noted the folded canvas on the roof. Mike was standing by, also Wakely. "Loaded scatterguns back of Angus and Pete, between them and the strongbox," Mike told his kinsman. "They got pistols too. Pete's is stuck in the back of his pants."

"Spare shot-gun in here," Judd informed the taller Texan. "And plenty room for your Winchester. I know you use two hand-guns. You fetch . . . ?"

"Yup, I'm packin' my second hogleg," nodded Stretch.

"So climb in and get comfortable," urged Judd. "Valentine, you still want the roof?"

"That's my spot," insisted Larry. He tossed his rifle up to the roof and, before raising a boot to the top of a wheel, offered Mike his left hand. They shook. "Don't bellyache, cousin. You keep wearin' that star, there'll be other times."

"I know I'll see you back in town," muttered Mike. "Wasn't any other bandit gang could lick you and Stretch, so why should the Duval bunch be any exception?"

Overhearing that, Reisner spoke

grimly; his was a harsh voice, matching his stubbled face and angry eyes.

"Let 'em do their worst. This time, *they* lose."

Larry raised a boot, reached for the baggage-rack and swung up and over onto the roof. He unfolded the tarp, lay prone and covered himself, while his partner joined Judd inside.

"All right, I guess we're ready," said Judd.

"All the luck, boys," offered the depot-boss.

"Keep an eye on the town till we get back, laddie," Munro called cheerily to his young colleague.

Mike nodded solemnly. Reisner kicked off his brake and growled at his three spans. The team moved off hauling the coach south along the alley to the outskirts; he then veered them toward the south trail.

"Thinkin' this's what Duval expects?" Stretch asked Judd.

"The story told for the benefit of the eavesdropper," said Judd, "is of a big

198

crew laying track far south of here for a spur line of the N and C Railroad — long overdue for a payday. The empty cashbox is supposed to contain thirty thousand in greenbacks."

"That ought to be bait enough," opined Stretch.

"We'll find out," Judd calmly predicted. "Before this day is through."

From under the front end of the tarp, Larry was already staring past the driver and guard, scanning the terrain ahead and to either side. And remembering the sad eyes of Dex Beech and three graves in the Pegrum County cemetery.

Neither Texan spared a thought for young Enoch, which was perhaps fortunate for their peace of mind. Right now, as unobtrusively as possible, taking care he would not be seen by Deputy Mike Valentine, the kid from Wyoming was making for the Triple J livery stable, toting his rifle and intending to saddle up, leave Gould City quietly and follow the bandit-baiters.

7

Blood Lust

TWO miles south of Gould City, Enoch wrestled with misgivings. So far, he was finding cover and using it, riding screening brush west of the stage route, raising no tell-tale dust and catching occasional glimpses of the coach a fair distance ahead. But would he continue to be so lucky? His was a simple plan. Keep the coach in sight and, when the bandits appeared, go to ground and draw a bead on one rider. It would be long-range, but he was a keen marksman, he could drop that one rider, the only one who wouldn't bother to conceal his face, that face being already known to the law.

But what if he were suddenly deprived of cover, no brush, no rock-clumps to shield him from view of the driver and guard? They could spot him. It would take only a quick backward glance by any of them, Larry maybe on the coach roof. They would call a halt. Larry would be furious with him, might even paddle his butt before ordering him back to town.

He didn't relish that humiliation, so he proceeded with care, hugging all the cover he could find — and hoping it would last long enough.

Inside the vehicle, Judd was calmly smoking his pipe. With the men up top on the alert, no reason he shouldn't engage the taller trouble-shooter in conversation.

"Not your first time?" he asked. "This kind of operation?"

"We've done it before," drawled Stretch. "I think, the last time, Larry did what he's doin' now, hid under a tarp on the roof." He worked his cigar to the side of his mouth and reminisced. "There was another time I recall, damned if we didn't use a dummy. Why, we even gave it a name. Shot-gun Sharkey."

"A dummy?" frowned Judd.

"Like you see in tailor shop windows, you know?" grinned Stretch. "Rigged in a suit, man-sized?"

"You dressed a dummy, fixed it beside the driver . . . ?"

"Well, hold-up artists ain't partial to buckshot, right? The guard, he's their first target. Sure, he looked plumb lifelike stuck up there. We bent his arms, made it look like he was cradlin' a scattergun. He drew plenty fire too."

"I suppose you and your friend've lost count of the running fights you've had with raiding parties."

"Uh huh. And all kinds of rigs. Sometimes a stagecoach, sometimes a freight wagon. There was a time, way back, us and some other fellers hid inside an ore wagon and drew a bunch of gold-thieves into one helluva showdown."

Studying Stretch's homely visage, Judd shook his head in bemusement.

"All seems natural to you two, doesn't it?" he remarked. "Year after year of wandering. The fights, the risks, the close calls. I've read every bulletin, every newspaper report and, as far back as ten years ago, I used to wonder how long you could keep it up. Other men — the kind I call normal — would've given up long before now. You know, Emerson, it could be said you and your partner've done more than your share, to put it mildly, of ridding the frontier of murderous riff-raff."

"If you said that to my partner," muttered Stretch, "he'd say there's still plenty riff-raff around, plenty mean hombres bedevilin' lawabidin' folks, not carin' a damn how many they kill or hurt. Mind you, Sheriff Judd suh, we don't go lookin' for 'em. We just keep runnin' into 'em."

"You came looking for them this time," argued Judd. "Looking for Blanco Duval's outfit, looking to wipe 'em out."

"Yeah, well, Larry told you why," said Stretch.

"Yes, the Diamond B rancher in Wyoming," nodded Judd. "The one whose sons were butchered by the Duval gang, a widower now."

"We figure Dex Beech has lost more'n an honest cattleman ought to lose," declared Stretch.

"He's only one," Judd pointed out. "Duval and his men've done a lot of killing."

"So?" challenged Stretch. "Why *wouldn't* we want to settle their hash?"

"I got no argument to that," said Judd. "He thrust his head out a window to call to Reisner and his deputy. "Anything?"

"Not yet," replied Munro. "But we could see some action any time. Our friend on the roof speaks of a feeling in his bones. That, I take it, is some kind of omen."

Judd withdrew his head and looked at Stretch, who gravely assured him,

"My ol' buddy's bones is scarce ever wrong."

Checking his watch, Judd calculated, "We've come a far trace from Gould City."

"Lucky for us it's a good trail," said Stretch. "That driver sure ain't sparin' the horses."

"Reisner's spoiling for a fight," said Judd. "He has his own score to settle with Duval."

For another mile, Enoch had to ride open country, fretting every yard of the way. He breathed a sigh of relief when his black pony carried him into a stand of timber.

Stretch, staring out his window, surveyed the terrain west.

"Quite a gap over there," he observed.

"It extends for miles," offered Judd. "The long rim of a high bluff. Not likely there'll ever be any mining of the area beyond. The cliff-face is too steep, just about perpendicular in fact."

Another mile. Larry, staring ahead, began a remark. "If I was a bushwacker cravin' a good stakeout . . . "

"I see what you mean," frowned Munro.

"Sure," grunted Reisner. "Them rocks, big 'uns and a lot of 'em. East of the trail."

"Less than thirty yards I'd say," muttered Munro. "Concealment for a heavy force of mounted men. Valentine, have you sighted something I've missed?"

"This could be the place," warned Larry. "Rocks throw shadows, but the shadow of a rock don't move, not fast anyway."

"All right," nodded Munro. "If you're sure you saw a moving shadow . . . "

"Not of a rock," growled Larry. "Of a horse."

Munro promptly called to his chief.

"It'll happen soon, Phin. The rocks ahead, left side."

Hearing that, Stretch made quick movements; his hands were suddenly hefting his matched .45s, cocked, and Judd was drawing back both hammers of his shot-gun. Reisner kept the rig

206

rolling fast, did not begin hauling back on his reins till the seven horsemen broke from the rocks to block the trail, six of them hooded, all seven aiming Colts, the blond man on the clean-limbed bay laughing harshly and triggering.

Reisner was applying the break when the bullet struck his breastplate. The impact jolted him and the metallic sound of it went unheard by the ambushers. His chest hurt, but the pain wasn't intense and he was well and truly conscious. Blacksmith Tebbut had saved his life. He slumped with his head lolling. "Want some of the same, guard?" chuckled the aptly nicknamed, pink-faced, pale-haired bandit.

"Don't shoot!" gasped Munro.

He dropped the empty shot-gun as though it had suddenly become red-hot.

"Now throw down that cashbox!" another man ordered.

With a fine show of apprehension, Munro reached behind him, grabbed at the strongbox and threw it down. He also grabbed and cocked his hideaway shot-gun and was turning and using it before the strongbox hit the dust.

The showdown was thunderous and bloody. A saddle was emptied by the double blast of the deputy's shot-gun. As the hooded-riders began scattering with their six-guns booming, Larry propped himself on his elbows with the tarp falling away from him, discharged his rifle and killed Duval's half-breed tracker, then cursed bitterly. At the first hint of resistance, the blond man on the bay had cut and run, leaving his companions to their fate.

Yelling ferociously, caring nought for .45 slugs coming too close for comfort, Reisner armed himself with the second shot-gun, discharged both barrels into the dust cloud raised by the hooves of milling horses, then tugged his six-guns from the back of his pants and sought targets.

Two bullets had spent themselves against Munro's steel vest; he too was cutting loose with a Colt now. From his window, Judd discharged a barrel at a moving target and missed. With his second shot, he sent a rider back-somersaulting over his mount's rump. A hooded horseman loomed on the west side of the stalled vehicle to trigger a slug that singed Stretch's whiskers. Stretch's right-hand Colt boomed in retaliation. The bandit keeled from his saddle with his hood bloody.

"The hell with it," Judd heard Stretch growl. "From in here, I can't get clear beads on the sonsabitches."

With that, he opened the rightside door and leapt out. No riders visible, so he dropped, crawled under the coach and came upright on its east side with his Colts roaring. Larry fired from the roof, his .45 jumping in his fist. He could see a fleeing rider and was eager to get this shootout over and done with, then give chase.

Judd followed Stretch's example, dropping from the coach with his Colt at the ready. By then, the dust was settling and five outlaw horses riderless. The sixth man, creased by the taller Texan, loosed a howl, dropped his pistol and toppled.

And that was Larry's cue to move.

"I'm headed after Duval!" he yelled as he clambered down.

Holstering his Colt, he ran to a quivering dun gelding and threw himself astride. Then he was kicking the animal to a gallop and heading westward in pursuit of the blond man on the bay.

"Damn!" raged Reisner. "Duval took off!"

"Relax, amigo," soothed Stretch. "No matter how hard he rides — or how far — he won't shake my partner off."

Munro and the driver rid themselves of their heavy vests and climbed down. Grim-faced, sheriff and deputy surveyed the sprawled losers.

"End of the Duval gang, Phin," muttered Munro, as Stretch began collecting fallen pistols. "Only one of 'em groaning. I believe the others . . ."

"The others," scowled Judd, "are *good* outlaws now."

Larry, urging his commandeered mount to greater speed, stared ahead and saw his quarry change direction. Duval made a sudden turn. He was riding south now, so Larry swung in that direction to head him off.

Was Duval in panic now? Maybe. He turned in his saddle to glance quickly to his left, so he had to have sighted his pursuer. Larry heard the report of his Colt and saw a spurt of dust kicked up a little way ahead; they were not yet in hand-gun range of each other. A few more minutes and he was closing the gap separating them and glimpsing Duval's reason for changing direction; quarry and pursuer now rode the rim of a bluff.

Duval fired over his shoulder, giving himself no time to take aim, a snap shot meant to discourage the rider dogging him, as if that were possible.

Relentlessly, eyes fixed on his quarry,

Larry kept coming. And then he saw the bay stumble and pitch forward, Duval hurtling over its head, the animal falling to the left, Duval to the right, crashing to the edge of the bluff. He didn't yell as he disappeared over the side. Tight-jawed, Larry eased his pace, letting the dun idle panting toward the bay, which now regained its feet, trembling, lathered.

He dismounted and ground-reined both animals, ears cocked to the diminishing sounds beyond and below the rim of the bluff, small rocks, rubble clattering down its face. Approaching the rim, noting the distance separating him from the mesas farther west, he warily dropped to all fours to crawl the rest of the way; to be upright at the edge of a sheer drop and looking downward could be an awesome experience, could cause dizziness. And he didn't need that.

Prone, he thrust his head over and stared down — and saw Duval.

The shelf was some ten feet down

and about four feet in width. Duval was sprawled on his back, looking up at him, hatless and with his holster empty. The empty holster was no surprise. Larry had sighted the six-gun on the ground beside the bay. Seeing Duval on that ledge *was* a surprise. And the defiant leer angered him.

Duval raised himself on an elbow, peered over the side of the shelf and chuckled.

"Lucky, lucky me. Long way down."

"A smart polecat knows when he's all through," muttered Larry. "Ledge looks strong enough to hold you. You can climb back up here if you move careful and with me helpin'. Or you can roll off and take a long fall. It's all one to me."

"Cold-hearted sonofabith, ain't you?" remarked Duval. He sat up, delved into a picket and found a cigar. "Got a match?" Larry held out a match between finger and thumb and let go. It fell on the blond man's chest. He took it, scratched it on his thumbnail and held it flaring to his stogie. "You don't look like no lawman. Tinhorn I'd reckon."

"Speakin' of cold-hearted sonsabitches," Larry said scathingly.

"Mean, huh?" grinned Duval. "And you don't give me any kind of chance. You help me up off of here and I hang, or I go over. You somebody I ought to know?"

"The name's Valentine," said Larry.

The grin broadened.

"I'll be damned! Valentine the do-gooder! Didn't recognize you and your stringbean partner when you stopped by Limbo Gulch." He puffed smoke and craned his neck, appraising Larry with increased interest. "You know, there should've been nine of us hit the coach from Gould City. You and your sidekicks cost me two good men at the Gulch, Duke Shaw and Tom Skimmer. What the hell, Valentine? What'd I ever do to you?"

"Nothin'," scowled Larry. "But I ain't forgettin' what you did in Wyomin'.

Remember the Diamond B raid?"

Duval's eyes narrowed.

"What about Diamond B?" he demanded.

"Can't remember 'em all, huh Duval?" Larry challenged. "All them you've butchered. Wasn't enough you gunned down Dex Beech's sons. His wife died of grief. You robbed him of his whole family and you don't care a damn."

The reaction sickened him. Duval gawked up at him incredulously, then burst into laughter.

"Beech — old Gentleman Dex? A wife and sons? It was *him* hired you and Emerson?"

"For this, he don't owe us a dime," growled Larry.

"Man, oh man!" Duval was still laughing. "Valentine, the smart-aleck trouble-shooter — played for a sucker! Well, by Judas, Dex sure fooled you. That's how he tricked you and your buddy into trackin' me down? More fool you. You're a jackass, Valentine, a soft touch and an easy mark. If

215

you believe what Dex told you, you'll believe *anything*!"

"In your spot, *I* wouldn't be laughin'," Larry retorted, but now his scalp was crawling and his gorge rising.

"Well. *I'm* laughin'," jeered Duval. "Dex never had no wife nor sired no kids. Up till five years ago, he was one of us. We all rode together, me, Dex, Ames and Cuttle, slick Nick Tresler. Me and Dex headed up a big outfit, I'm tellin' you, hit a lot of banks and stage lines all over the northwest," He puffed on his cigar and grinned derisively, savoring Larry's shock. "Then we split up. Dex was always the gent, cravin' respectability, you know? Had a hankerin' to take his share of our loot and set himself up as a cattleman, Nick and Ames and Cuttle with him. And they did just fine. A little while back, I paid 'em a visit."

"You made it to Diamond B without runnin' into a lawman?" frowned Larry.

216

"Travelled at night," shrugged Duval. "Read in the Pegrum County newspaper that Dex was gettin' to be a big man in that territory and mighty popular with the civic fathers. Seems he got all the respectability he craved — even got himself all set to marry the mayor's sister. How d'you like that, hot shot? Proves how high a smart thief can reach. I was a mite short of ready cash around that time, so I figured that'd be my chance for a handout — and I don't mean nickels and dimes."

"Beech wasn't happy to see you," guessed Larry, tight-reining his fury.

"If you could've seen the look on his face," chuckled Duval. "As if he was seein' a ghost. Then I told him he needn't fret about me. I'd keep his secret, wouldn't be any of his high and mighty friends ever learn he used to ride owlhoot and did his share of killin' in the old days, just so long as he did right by an old compadre. Two thousand I collected from him. Easy money." Abruptly, he stopped chuckling, his expression changed. "Guess I shook him some, huh? He decided I was too dangerous, maybe I'd make him pay more. So he conned you and you fell for that bull about a dead wife and sons and that's why you hunted me."

"And found you," Larry said grimly. "Enough palaver, Duval. You jumpin', or climbin'?"

"I guess I'll climb," Duval decided.

Before rising, he darted a glance downward and winced. He got to his feet slowly and turned to hug the cliff-face. His ascent was begun carefully. He found foot and hand holds and climbed six feet without mishap. A rock came loose as his right hand closed over it. He grasped it and leaned against the cliff-face and his inane snigger irritated Larry. He got another foothold and, again, raised himself.

"Give me your hand," ordered Larry, reaching down with his own.

Duval gripped Larry's hand.

"You strong enough to . . . ?"

"I can do it," said Larry.

As he hauled, he came to one knee, his muscles straining. Duval's head and shoulders appeared above the rim and he eased himself over and Larry released his hand and struggled upright and so did Duval and Larry was only half-ready for Duval's next move. He bared his teeth and hurled the fist-sized rock.

Larry ducked and backstepped hastily. The rock hurtled over his head and, in backstepping, he lost his footing and fell. He was sprawling and Duval snarling triumphantly, whisked a knife from the sheath concealed by his jacket. On his back, Larry caught a blurred impression of the killer leaping at him with the gleaming blade raised high for a death-thrust. He readied himself to block the downswing, to capture the wrist of the hand gripping the knife and then, from somewhere far to his right, he heard the echo of a rifle-shot.

Duval was atop him, pinning him,

but there was no cry of pain; he was a dead weight, his face pressed against his right shoulder. He turned his head and, with a chill in his belly, studied the hand still gripping the knife's hilt. Its blade was embedded in the ground between his left side and his out-flung arm.

Grimacing, he rolled to his right, let the body flop, then rose, staring down at it. He could see the bullet-hole a few inches under the left armpit. Safe bet the slug had entered between rib-bones and penetrated to the heart. A slow clip-clop of hooves announced the approaching rider. He turned to stare northward, expecting to see his partner straddling the horse of another dead outlaw. But no. It wasn't Stretch. It was Enoch Hesky astride his prized black colt.

He stood arms akimbo, waiting for the youth to reach him. Enoch arrived, reined up and put his troubled eyes on the dead man.

"That's . . . ?"

"Yeah, Duval," nodded Larry. "Some helluva sharpshooter you are, kid."

"Is he . . . ?"

"Dead as he'll ever be."

"Larry, I had to do it. I was a long ways back, but . . . "

"I know it was long-range."

"But I had to do it. I saw you help him up from down there and — honestly — I didn't draw a bead till he pulled the knife. He jumped you and — I couldn't just let him . . . !"

"You ain't supposed to be here," Larry reminded him.

"Sure," sighed Enoch. "You gave me an order. I ought to be back in Gould City."

"Can't cuss you out, can I?" mused Larry, shrugging resignedly. "Can't cuss a kid who just saved my life."

"I really did — did I? frowned Enoch. "I mean — it was that close?"

"It was that close," Larry assured him. "So I owe you. Muchas gracias, amigo, but I'm gonna hand you some advice you better heed — for your

221

own sake. Don't ever brag of savin' Valentine's life. There's some that wouldn't appreciate it. In a lot of places, there's soreheads who wish I was dead, Stretch too."

"Right now, I don't feel much like bragging anyway," said Enoch. "Hell, I've killed two men, and I'm only sixteen."

"Earned yourself the bounty on Duval too," said Larry. "And what's a green kid like you gonna do with five thousand dollars?"

"Me?" blinked Enoch.

"It's what you had your mind set on, right?" challenged Larry. "Nail Blanco Jack Duval, collect the reward?"

"Holy Moses!" breathed Enoch. "Five thousand dollars" He gnawed at his underlip. "Well, I don't know what I'll do with it — yet. It's something I'll have to think about." He worked up a hesitant grin. "Good answer?"

"The best," Larry said approvingly. "All right, kid, time to get back to the others. No, you stay mounted. I've done this many a time, don't need no help."

He retrieved the dead outlaw's pistol and shoved it in his waistband, lifted the body and hung it across its saddle, then remounted the dun and took the other animal's rein. With Enoch keeping pace, he started back for the stage route and the scene of the showdown.

The only survivor of the Duval gang had been accorded rough surgery by Reisner, while Stretch and Munro secured bodies to horses, some of which would carry double. Judd collected weapons, retrieved the empty strongbox and loaded them onto the coach. The wounded man was unconscious. Reisner, staring westward, voiced a name bitterly.

"Duval."

"Don't fret, Pete," said Judd. "Valentine'll catch up with him. What do you say, Emerson?"

"The way Larry feels about Duval," drawled Stretch, "he ain't lettin' up."

"They're coming now," announced Munro.

From the west, the three horses approached, two toting riders, one a draped body. The stage driver was confused.

"Only one of us took off after Duval," he frowned. "Who's on the charcoal?"

"Hell's sakes," grouched Stretch. "The Kid."

"I told him . . ." began Judd.

"Larry told him too," nodded Stretch.

Reisner shook off his confusion and concentrated with grim satisfaction on the third animal and its burden.

"That's all I care about," he muttered. "It's got to be Duval's carcass hung over that critter."

"The northwest'll be the better for his passing, Phin," said Munro.

"I used to wonder how long it'd take," said Judd. "But I had faith in our strategy, especially after these trouble-shooters threw in with us."

When they arrived, Larry forestalled reprimands against Enoch by bluntly accounting, "The kid nailed Duval. Better nobody bawls him out."

"He disobeyed orders," Judd said, but mildly.

"Right," nodded Larry. "And, if he hadn't, Duval might've got me with a knife."

He dismounted, lit a cigar and recounted his pursuit of the boss-outlaw, telling of Duval's mishap and his helping him to safety, then Duval's murderous attack and his sudden death, thanks to Enoch's long-range marksmanship. Not a word of his exchange with the killer, the things said while Duval lay on the shelf on the cliff-face, was repeated. No concern of the Gould City law, he had decided. His and Stretch's unfinished business. And finish it they would. As they made ready to return to the county seat, Munro began a question.

"The reward on Duval, will you share it or . . . ?"

"It happened like I said," declared Larry. "Duval was the kid's kill, so the kid collects the whole bundle." He frowned at Enoch, who had not dismounted, and at Judd. "Phin, about the Gould City newspaper. It's up to the kid how much he wants to tell a scribbler and whether he wants his picture in the paper, but we'd take it kindly if you don't mention our names."

"How about Webb and Terhune?" asked Judd.

"Sure, Webb and Terhune," shrugged Larry. "Them names won't mean nothin' to Mister Oliver Aiken."

"And we'll stay far clear of him anyway," said Stretch.

It was decided Munro and the youth would lead the laden horses and the Texans travel inside the coach with the sheriff. Before climbing aboard, Larry matched stares with Enoch.

"Has to be your own decision, kid," he said. "You get the money, and that's fair enough. You could get to be famous too. Big reputation. The gun that stopped Blanco Jack Duval.

But, before you make up your mind, think some, huh? Think of what a big reputation's meant to my partner and me."

"Yes." Enoch nodded slowly. "I guess I'll be careful how I answer questions. And I'm not sure I want my picture in a newspaper anyway."

Reisner climbed to the seat to kick off his brake and wheel the team. The coach rolled north tagged by Munro and Enoch leading the animals carrying the one wounded and six dead desperadoes. Inside the vehicle, Judd filled and lit his pipe, relaxed and studied the tall men sharing the seat opposite.

"I don't enjoy this feeling often enough — I guess few law-men do," he remarked. "A band of outlaws, real bad ones, finally accounted for. Duval and his killers were at large too long, far too long."

"None of 'em last forever," Larry said moodily.

"While Duval was trapped on that

ledge, before you helped him up from there," said Judd, "was there no talk? You said nothing to each other?"

"I gave him his choice," said Larry. "Climb up or roll over."

"That's all?" asked Judd.

"There was somethin' else," said Larry. "He complained I cost him two good men in Limbo Gulch. Seems they weren't a tinhorn and a miner, the sharper I shot, the horse-thief the kid downed."

"Which explains why there were seven raiders this time instead of nine," mused Judd. "And it also confirms your hunch about Limbo Gulch. It *was* their hideout."

"What'll happen about the Gulch?" prodded Stretch.

"Well, a jasper wearing a badge and collaborating with outlaws, the saloon-keeper aware of their identity, those two and several others . . . " began Judd.

"Every soul there," insisted Stretch.

"Right," nodded Judd. "I believe I'll

leave the Limbo Gulch people to the tender mercy of the Federal authorities. There's an office of the U.S. Marshal at the territorial capital. I'll mail him a report, a long one. In due course, Federals will visit the Gulch. I predict those who were in close cahoots with the Duval bunch will suffer for it, one way or another."

"Runt, what're we gonna do about the kid?" demanded Stretch.

"Take him home to Maddenville I guess," said Larry. "About the bounty, Phin, can you take care of what's got to be done?"

"I'll help the boy fill out the claim form and send it to the appropriate authority," offered Judd. "And I'm sure I can persuade him it'd be best for him to go home. Safest way for him to collect would be to arrange a draft on a Maddenville bank in his name."

"That'd be better, a whole lot better," opined Stretch.

He eyed his partner sidelong. "You feelin' poorly, ol' buddy?"

"I'm fine," said Larry.

Stretch didn't push it. They had ridden together for all of two decades. He could sense Larry's changes of mood and, right now, he knew he was sitting beside one seething Texan, a human powderkeg with a short fuse. Something had happened, something more than another close call. In his own good time, Larry would confide in him. Meanwhile, he could wait.

Temporary deprivation of the use of his right arm did not prevent Judd's junior deputy from being first to reach the returning winners and losers. He was pacing beside a saddled horse at the south edge of town when they appeared in the distance and at once swung astride and rode out to meet them. To Mike's credit, he used his eyes and did not irritate his boss with superfluous questions.

Riding level with the coach, he asked, "Orders?"

"Yes," Judd answered from the nearside window. "We have only one live prisoner. We'll need a doctor to see to his wound. Angus'll hand him over to Saul and arrange transfer of the bodies to the funeral parlor. What I want you to do, Mike, is stall Oley Aiken. Be polite about it. Just head for his office and ask him to wait an hour before coming to the county jail. I'll have a statement for him by then. It's all right to tell him the Duval gang was wiped out this morning."

"You need an hour — right," nodded Mike.

"It'll take that long for us to get the affidavits written and signed and witnessed," explained Judd. "Then your cousin and his friend'll want to leave by the rear door to avoid running into a mighty inquisitive newspaperman."

"I'll take care of Aiken," Mike promised. Before heeling his mount, he peered into the coach. "Larry . . . ?"

"Fine," Larry called to him, and added a lie. "Never felt better."

The younger deputy rode on to reach the office of the *Chronicle* a full ten minutes before the coach rolled into Main Street. At Judd's urging, the Texans and Enoch made straight for the law office. The sheriff and his senior deputy joined them there a short time later, Munro toting the wounded prisoner and with a doctor at his heels. The routine of committing all statements to paper began after the medico went to work on his patient under Greeber's watchful eye.

When all affidavits were signed and witnessed, Judd filled out the claim form and offered Enoch a pen.

"Sign on the bottom line, son. You do have a name, right? Other than just 'Kid'?"

"Yes, sir," said Enoch.

Judd studied the signature.

"Enoch Hesky. Well, young Enoch, big day for you. I just hope, when a Maddenville bank advises you of the arrival of the draft, you'll have made some intelligent plans about how best to use your money."

"Like I promised, I'm gonna do a

lot of thinking about it," said Enoch.

"I take it you heroes'll leave us early tomorrow," Judd remarked. "Stop by and say goodbye on your way out by all means. And now Angus'll open the back door for you. Aiken could arrive any moment. I don't think Mike can hold him much longer."

By a roundabout route, Enoch and the tall men made for the Palace Hotel, Larry still tight-reining his fury.

8

Retribution

IN their room, Larry rid himself of hat and coat and began pacing, eyes gleaming, mouth set in a hard line. Stretch helped himself to a chair, smoked and waited.

"Any time you're ready, runt," he offered.

"We've been used!" breathed Larry.

"Used?" frowned Stretch.

"Lied to, played for suckers by a bastard no better'n Duval himself, old companero of Duval's in fact," scowled Larry. "I'm talkin' about Beech." Stretch loosed a low whistle. "We won't find them graves in the Pegrum County cemetery, Madeline Beech, her sons Ritchie and Hollis. There never was no Madeline Beech. That sonofabitch never had no wife

— though he's got weddin' plans now."

Stretch grimaced in disgust and slumped lower in his chair.

"You and Duval palavered plenty," he guessed. "You didn't tell Phin everything you learned from him."

"It's 'tween us and Beech," declared Larry. "And three others we met at Diamond B, the ramrod Tresler and them Beech called the best hands on his payroll, Ames and Cuttle."

"All right, tell it all," urged Stretch.

Larry stopped pacing, drew up a chair and repeated almost word for word the taunt voiced by Duval, plus Beech's plans for his future. It was now the taller Texan's turn to curse, and he did so fluently.

Subsiding a little, Larry remarked, "It's somethin' we've always known about thieves and killers. We learned it many a long year ago."

"What somethin'?" asked Stretch.

"No matter how smart they are, no matter how cunning, they make mistakes — dumb mistakes," muttered Larry.

"Ain't that the truth," Stretch agreed. "Beech took us for granted. He looked for us to run Duval to ground. There'd be a mess of shootin' and Duval'd get his, die on his feet. That's what he wanted. Us shuttin' Duval's mouth — permanent. The one thing he never counted on . . . "

"Was Duval gettin' time to talk to us," nodded Larry.

"I was never as smart-brained as you," sighed Stretch.

"Hell, runt, I felt sorry for him, believed everything he told us. I respected him, damned if I didn't."

"Am I any smarter'n you?" growled Larry. "You think he didn't have *me* fooled?"

"We just naturally trusted him," Stretch sourly complained. "And, you know, if he could make us believe in him, maybe we're gettin' old and careless — a little stupid maybe."

"Let's quit feelin' sorry for ourselves,"

frowned Larry. "That ain't our style, and we got a score to settle."

"Startin' tomorrow, we head back to Wyomin'," guessed Stretch. "Take the kid home, head on to Castleton and get rid of the whiskers, and then . . . "

"Pegrum next stop," said Larry. "That's where we end it. Diamond B, the county seat, somewhere in that territory."

"County sheriff totes a grudge against Texans," warned Stretch.

"Who says so?" retorted Larry. "A liar name of Beech. Best stay far clear of the county seat, he said, and now we know why. He couldn't risk us nosin' around that town, maybe wanderin' through the cemetery . . . "

"Where there's supposed to be three graves which ain't there," nodded Stretch.

"And maybe hearin' he's fixin' to get married," sneered Larry, "only five months after he buried his wife and sons." He swore, then shook his head impatiently, "All right, enough of chewin' it over. We know what we got to do — and we'll sure as hell do it."

★ ★ ★

The trouble-shooters did think to say their goodbyes to Sheriff Judd and Larry's kinsman before riding out next morning. Amply provisioned, they pushed west for the border and Maddenville with Enoch who, after Gould City was well to their rear, self-consciously confided he had come to a decision regarding his future.

"You don't have to tell us — you old bounty-hunter you," drawled Stretch. "But, if you want to . . . "

"If it sounds like a dumb idea to us, we'll damn soon say so," growled Larry.

"That's why I *want* to tell you," offered Enoch. "I need your opinion because everything you ever taught me made a lot of sense."

"So let's hear it," invited Stretch.

"Well, like Uncle Gus and most Maddenville folks say, I'm clumsy in most ways," said Enoch. "I can ride and I'm a fair shot. Didn't seem I was much use at anything else but, last night, I remembered something."

"Somethin' you're good at?" prodded Stretch.

"Maybe," Enoch said guardedly. "I won't know for sure till I ask Mister Fenrick."

"You know what comes next." Larry was controlling his exasperation. "One of us says 'Who's Mister Fenrick?' and you tell us."

"Micah Fenrick, he's the gunsmith at Maddenville," explained Enoch. "*Only* gunsmith at Maddenville. You see, a couple of months back, there was something wrong with my rifle. Well, I didn't have cash enough for . . ."

"Yeah, you were poor back then," nodded Larry. "Didn't have five thousand dollars."

"Couldn't ask Mister Fenrick to fix my rifle for free," continued Enoch.

"So I kind of tinkered with it. Got a screw-driver, worked on it a while and must've found what was wrong and fixed it."

"Must've fixed it right," Larry readily agreed. "That Winchester's got to be in prime order, else you couldn't've scored on Duval from so far off."

"So there's a chance do you think?" suggested Enoch. "I could have what it takes to learn the trade, get to be a gunsmith?"

"How do *you* feel about that?" countered Larry.

"I'd sure like to try," declared Enoch. "Mister Fenrick runs his place all by himself. I could help out while he's teaching me and maybe we'll get along, maybe he'll be patient. Not like Mister Engle or Uncle Gus or the carpenter or the rancher or any of the others. You see, I never worked for Mister Fenrick. And I could offer to invest in the business, couldn't I? I plan on giving Uncle Gus some cash for improvements at his barber shop because he and Aunt Dorrie took me in and I've been a burden on 'em. I'll keep most of my money in the bank and I could buy into the gunsmithery if Mister Fenrick decides I could learn the business."

He eyed the tall men, eager for their opinion. They hesitated, not relishing the responsibility of helping decided his future. He wasn't just the pesky kid any more; his bankroll exceeded theirs.

Larry finally suggested, "Talk it over with Uncle Gus, the sheriff too, before you put it to the gunsmith. By the time we make Maddenville, the big news'll spread all over. If Maddenville's got a newspaper."

"Sure," said Enoch. "The *Madden County Dispatch*."

"Well, what with the telegraph and all, you'll come home to some kind of welcome," predicted Larry. "The sheriff'll allow you ain't as dumb as he thought, or maybe you've aged some. You ask what he thinks, him and Uncle Gus, they'll appreciate you wantin' their advice and maybe get the idea you're smarter'n when you quit town."

"Thanks," grinned Enoch. "That's how I'll do it."

When Maddenville was reached, it was at once obvious that news of Enoch's success had preceded them. A hero's welcome? Not exactly. But as they rode the main street, Enoch was the focus of attention. The Texans, to their secret gratification, were barely noticed. People eyed Enoch with increased interest, with curiosity and cautious admiration, also incredulously. His uncle and aunt emerged from the barber shop; Larry got the impression *they* were the *most* incredulous. The editor of the *Dispatch* requested Enoch grant him an interview and, by the time he was dismounting, a crowd was converging.

He stared up at the Texans, suddenly realizing, "I'll probably never ever seen you again. I bet you'll ride on rightaway, so I'll have no time for thanking you for all you've . . . "

"One of us got plenty to thank *you* for," Larry reminded him.

They leaned from their saddles to offer their hands. Enoch shook with them and, soon afterward, lost sight of them. His uncle and aunt, Sheriff O'Gorman and Deputy Harroway, a lot of people, a whole crowd, surrounded him to offer congratulations. The day they returned to Castleton, the trouble-shooters felt an urge to bee-line for the first barber shop sighted. They stifled that urge long enough to look in on Tex Harrick who welcomed them eagerly and congratulated them on having achieved their purpose.

"We got the news a couple days ago," he announced while pumping their hands. "Mind now, it didn't surprise me. What you boys set, you finish, right?"

"We try, Tex," shrugged Stretch.

"Gonna hold to your word, I hope?" pleaded Tex. "Have supper with Cassie and me tonight?"

"Count on us," Larry assured him. "But, right now, there's somethin' we got to get rid of."

"Not just the whiskers," said Stretch. "These dude outfits too. We'll be fetchin' 'em back to you, amigo."

"Your regular rigouts're ready when you want 'em," offered Tex. "Washed clean. I even dusted off your tiles."

At the barber shop, the tall men bought haircuts and gratefully submitted to scissors and razor. The beards had served their purpose; they were glad to be rid of them.

Lonz Ackerby inspected the dapple and the strawberry roan while the Texans responded to the nickered greetings of the animals left in his care. Larry's sorrel and Stretch's pinto were well rested and in excellent condition. The Texans informed him they'd be leaving in the morning.

After checking into a hotel for their overnight stay, they stopped by the clothing store again and took pleasure in changing to their range rig.

"Feels a whole lot better," Stretch enthused, buckling on his double-holstered shellbelt.

"I'll bet," nodded Tex. "Looks better too. Now you look like who you are. So what're you gonna do between now and suppertime?"

"Head on back to the hotel and flop," declared Larry. "We checked in as Webb and Terhune and we're gonna lay low till sundown. You got a newspaper here and the hombre that runs it is one citizen we don't craze to parley with."

"Can't say I blame you," said Tex. "It'd go to his head. The way Burt Strauss'd write about you, he'd have his readers believing Duval had a dozen guns backing him. He's the kind of newspaperman stretches the truth."

"Him and most of 'em," complained Larry. "See you later, Tex."

Supper with the Harricks was, in every way, a pleasant respite from recent hectic activity. Cassie Harrick served a fine meal and was an amiable hostess. Her husband and the men he so admired talked affectionately of early years in their home-state, traded tall stories and, by the time supper ended, had her laughing helplessly.

"I declare I'll never understand," she smiled when they were taking their leave. "After all the hardship you've suffered, the danger you've known — and all the fighting — it doesn't seem natural you can still make jokes."

"Our guests're a whole lot smarter than they look, honey," Tex said wistfully. "They know the saddest men are those who've lost their sense of humor. And these bucks'll never be *that* sad."

In the morning, after a substantial breakfast, the drifters checked out of the hotel and hefted their gear along to the livery stable to ready their mounts for the journey to Pegrum county. The proprietor, watching them secure cinches and attach sheathed rifles, saddlebags and packrolls, was moved to remark, "I'm might thankful I'm not him."

"Not who?" asked Stretch.

"Whoever your partner hankers to square accounts with," muttered Ackerby.

"It shows?" Larry forced a grin.

"It shows," nodded Ackerby.

The tall men led their animals into the street, raised boots to stirrups and swung astride. Before making for a side street they could follow to the western outskirts, they rode past the Harrick store to trade farewell waves with a fellow-Texan and doff their Stetsons to his wife.

With Castleton a mile behind them and their mounts moving briskly, Stretch soberly declared, "That was right sociable, a real friendly visit, but now we got unfinished business."

"If you ain't as sore as me, you ought to be," muttered Larry.

"I'm good and mad," scowled Stretch. "I keep rememberin' how sorry I felt for him, how I believed all his lies."

"Duval said they all did plenty killin'," recalled Larry. "Beech, Tresler, Ames, Cuttle. And now Beech's all set to take a wife — the mayor's sister no less."

"After that?" mused Stretch.

"Maybe he gets to be an alderman, one of the big shots runnin' that territory," Larry said bitterly. "Hell, he could end up in his brother-in-law's chair, be mayor of Pegrum some day." An ugly thought came to him now; he voiced it in disgust. "I wonder how many more of 'em got away with it."

"You mean bandidos with a little education and a lot of ambition," guessed Stretch.

"Right," nodded Larry. "How many killers've quit outlawry, taken their loot to some new territory and used it to start a store, a hotel — or a big spread like Diamond B? They gunned bank cashiers, lawmen, stagecoach guards, regular citizens, and got away clear, lived to make a new start."

"And no badge-toter gettin' wise to

'em," said Stretch. "Because, every time they went a'raidin', they covered their faces good."

"Could be a lot of 'em," complained Larry. "But not Beech," said Stretch.

"Not Beech," echoed Larry.

Noon of a fine, clear day in Wyoming, they camped a little way from their route and made lunch of roasted jackrabbit. They had their bearings, were recognizing landmarks and knew they were about to enter Pegrum County and the direction they should travel from here to reach the Beech ranch.

It was around 2.30 p.m. when they crossed Diamond B range, skirting grazing beeves tended by herders who recognized them and waved in friendly fashion. They returned those waves and assumed most of the crew were blissfully ignorant of their boss's past.

When they rode into the yard fronting the ranch-house, the only man to greet them was the chuck-boss. Approaching from his cook-shack, he nodded affably.

"I remember you boys. You over-nighted here a while back."

"Yup, that's us," said Stretch.

"Where's the boss?" asked Larry. "And the ramrod, and Ames and Cuttle?"

"In town," offered the chuck-boss. "Them three're old buddies of the boss. Where he goes, they go. Big celebration in the county seat tonight. They're gonna make it official."

"That so?" prodded Larry.

"Mayor Denning's throwin' a party at the Commercial Hotel," he was told. "His sister's birthday Miss Fran, that fine lady. Double celebration. They're gonna announce her betrothal to Mister Beech and name the weddin' date."

"Sounds like a lot of fun," Larry said poker-faced. "Well, we like a good celebration too. Whichaway to town?"

The chuck-boss gave directions and predicted they should reach Pegrum around sundown. They thanked him and rode away, postponing comments until they were on the trail they would

250

follow to their destination.

"Bad timin'?" frowned Stretch.

"*Good* timin'," insisted Larry. "Fine lady, the chuck-boss calls her. So we're doin' her a kindness."

It was a well-settled town bigger than Maddenville, more of a size with Gould City, South Dakota. Upon their arrival, they made for a livery stable, failing to notice a thin man in a townsuit taking more than a casual interest in them. He was loitering by the bar entrance when they turned their mounts over to a stablehand and made their enquiry. The stablehand replied they would find the Diamond B boss at the Commercial Hotel and that he had seen Nick Tresler and his companions enter the Appaloosa Saloon an hour before.

They walked to the saloon with the thin man tagging them, his coat buttoned, his derby set square on his dome, his eyes alert. Reaching the Appaloosa, they nudged the batwings open and moved in. And at once spotted Tresler, Ames and Cuttle sharing a table by the southside wall. The ramrod greeted them effusively.

"Valentine, Emerson, welcome back. Well, you really did it, huh? Took care of Blanco Jack once and for all. It was in the newspaper . . . "

"You ought to be mournin' him." Larry spoke so sharply, so accusingly, that other drinkers began edging clear. The tall men stood side by side, fifteen yards from the seated trio.

"Mournin' him?" frowned Ames.

"Before a bullet shut his mouth, Duval did a lot of talkin'," declared Larry. "You've been straight since the old gang broke up, you three — and Beech."

"But it wasn't always that way, was it?" challenged Stretch. "Duval bragged of the old days."

"Named you," growled Larry. "Told of all the killin' and lootin'." Left-handed, he gestured brusquely. "Just rise up, shuck your hardware and walk out with us. We're takin' you to the law."

First to rally from the shock, Tresler made two fast moves. He triggered at Larry from under the tabletop and, with his other hand, flung a bottle to distract the challengers. The bullet tore the left leg of Larry's Levis but only burned his flesh. He filled his hand and Stretch had no option but to follow suit; Ames and Cuttle were upright with their guns out. The Texans promptly cocked and fired and those two were sent hurtling against the wall, dead on their feet. Larry was more than ready to deal with Tresler, now leaping to his feet, but now another gun barked and Tresler dropped his Colt and lurched, clamping left hand to right arm. He was in agony and irate.

"*Damn* Duval!" he cried. "Dex paid him to keep his mouth shut!"

Pain and fury will do it time and time again, Stretch reflected. In that condition, many a trapped rogue had damned himself and others by an impulsive outburst. Now, haggard and trembling, Tresler cursed in frustration, while Larry glanced over his shoulder. To whip out his armpit-holstered .38 Smith & Wesson, the skinny man had unbuttoned his coat, revealing the six-pointed star fixed to his vest.

"I'll take over from here," he told the Texans. "Appreciate your help, but everything gets done official now." He holstered his pistol. "You don't have to identify yourselves. Riordan's my name, county sheriff."

Grim-eyed, the Texans ejected their spent shells and reloaded. Riordan picked up Tresler's gun and began prodding him toward the entrance. En route, he called to a barkeep to have some of his customers remove the dead men to the funeral parlor. The tall men automatically followed him out and kept pace with him and the pain-wracked prisoner.

There was no talk. On their way to the county law office and jail, they passed a brightly lit triple-storey building dominating a corner opposite, the Commercial Hotel.

A deputy rose from his desk, frowning, as they entered. Riordan ordered him to fetch a doctor and gestured for the turnkey to put Tresler in a cell. With the Texans, he was polite, but business-like. He motioned them to chairs, took a bottle and glasses from his desk drawer and poured three shots of rye.

"Was that a bluff?" he demanded after seating himself. "Or did Jack Duval name those four as old outlaw buddies of his before he stopped a bullet?"

"Duval really shot off his mouth," Larry assured him.

"But you didn't think to pass on what you heard to the Dakota law," accused Riordan. "I know it wasn't your bullet stopped Duval. Some kid name of Hesky. I read about it. Be straight with me, Valentine. You wanted it to be personal, just you and Emerson nailing the four of them?"

"We don't like bein' used," muttered Stretch.

"Used by who?" demanded Riordan. "Come on, talk to me."

Larry drained his glass, shrugged resignedly and fished out his makings. In the time it took him to roll, light and half-smoke a cigarette, he repeated to Riordan his motive for hunting the Duval gang, the lies by which Beech had won the sympathy of two veteran outlaw-fighters. By the time he was butting his cigarette, the lawman had heard his clear recollection of every word uttered by Duval in those long minutes before Larry hauled him to safety, almost at the cost of his own life. During this, the deputy returned, ushered a local medico into the cell-block and loitered, listening, trading frowns with his chief.

"And now . . . " Stretch sounded keenly disappointed, "I guess the law *really* takes over."

"If you heroes are as reasonable as you're supposed to be, you know I can't keep my backside in this chair and let you march up to the Commercial

Hotel for a showdown with Dexter Beech," said Riordan. "Well, is it all that important to your injured pride? One of you has to shoot him? Forget it. I doubt he's carrying a gun. What do you care, so long as justice is done? The statements you'll sign and the confession I'll get from Tresler . . . "

"If . . . " began Stretch.

"No if," retorted Riordan. "Tresler will confess. He'll be glad to by the time I'm through with him." He grinned mirthlessly. "You tumbleweeds can be ruthless when it suits you. But so can I, believe me."

"Believe him," the deputy advised the Texans. "I wouldn't be in Tresler's boots for all the gold in California."

"We don't have to delay picking Beech up, Gene," Riordan told the deputy. "We'll call in a JP after Beech is filling a cell and have Valentine's statement notarized." He rose abruptly. "We'll do it now. Valentine, you and your partner are welcome to come along, if I have your word you'll keep your hardware holstered."

"You got it," said Larry.

When they followed Sheriff Riordan and Deputy Murfries into the luxuriously appointed lobby of Pegrun's best hotel, a well-dressed quartet stood in a congenial group, trading friendly remarks, smoking Havanas — Beech, the mayor and two local councilmen. Sighting the Texans, Beech's jovial expression changed, but only for a moment.

"Glad you came back," he beamed, advancing on them with hand extended. "I hoped for a chance to congratulate you personally."

"Go to hell," scowled Larry.

"You lyin' skunk," growled Stretch.

"Use your irons, Gene," ordered Riordan. With Beech in shock, Murfries easily manacled his wrists. The sheriff then addressed the dumbfounded Mayor Ralph Denning. "He's under arrest for armed robberies and murders committed before he came to this territory, Mayor Denning, I'm sorry, believe me, especially for Miss Frances."

"Thunderation!" gasped Denning.

"It's a mistake, Ralph!" Beech said desperately.

"*Your* mistake!" snarled Larry.

"Something that never crossed your mind, Beech," said Riordan. "With Valentine and Emerson running him to ground, you assumed Duval would die fast. But that's not how it was. He spilled it all to Valentine, enough damning information to guarantee you'll be convicted. The rope or the rest of your life in prison — either way, you'll pay."

It was 8.30 that night before the Texans were free to find a restaurant and dig into a delayed supper. They had done everything required of them by the conscientious sheriff Riordan, tendered full statements, appended their signatures and seen the affidavits duly witnessed and notarized. Riordan had evidence aplenty.

"Probably scarin' hell out of Tresler right now," opined Stretch. "Skinny

259

jasper, that Riordan. Ain't much of him, but he's plenty salty."

"Even without our statements, he's got Beech cold," said Larry. "Tresler, Stretch. We've run into his kind before. When the chips're down, they think only of their own skin."

"He'll keep on blabbin', tell the sheriff anything, hopin' the judge'll give him a break?" frowned Stretch. "Is he dumb enough to believe that?"

"You could make book on it," muttered Larry.

"Yeah, well, it's all over," shrugged. Stretch. "Nothin' else for us to do. We can quit this town soon as we want, Riordan said. So, you want to ride soon as we've ate?"

"What's our rush?" Larry sounded weary. "We might's well bunk in a hotel tonight and quit in the mornin'. Quien sabe? It could be the last time we'll sleep in regular beds for a long time, for all we know.

They had eaten their fill and were drinking coffee when Stretch winced uneasily and said, "Maybe it wasn't right, us lettin' the kid tag along with us. He's five thousand dollars richer and he ain't dry behind the ears. We made him famous, runt, but can he handle that?"

"He's got Uncle Gus and Aunt Dorrie," said Larry. "And the sheriff and a lot of people keepin' an eye on him. I figure they'll steer him right. What the hell? We gonna worry about him the rest of our lives?"

This night, they made good use of soft beds, sleeping deeply a full nine hours. In the morning, after checking out, they ate breakfast at the cafe opposite the livery stable, after which they trudged across to the barn to ready the sorrel and pinto for the trail.

Any trail would do, they were thinking, when they tipped the stable-hand, led their horses into the street and got mounted.

They were short on coffee, tobacco and a few other necessaries, so sauntered their horses to a general store. Having made their purchases, they continued on along the main street, drawing little attention from locals out and about until the disheveled woman stumbled into the path. They reined up.

"*Damn you!*" she cried.

She wore an expensive gown, but no hat. Her hair was in disarray, her face flushed, her eyes wild. Plainly, the lady was much the worse for liquor. And she was heaping curses on them, accusing them of ruining her life. Passers-by paused to gape and then, while their scalps crawled, a harassed man they recognized as Mayor Denning appeared on the scene, took her arm and began leading her away.

"Happy birthday to me . . . !" she screamed.

They winced as they rode on, making for Pegrum's outskirts.

"The lady that . . . ?" began Stretch.

"That was gonna be Mrs Dexter Beech — who else?" Larry muttered through clenched teeth. "*Another* loser. C'mon, let's get the hell out of here."

FIGHTING RAMROD
Charles N. Heckelmann

Most men would have cut their losses, but Frazer counted the bullets in his guns and said he'd soak the range in blood before he'd give up another inch of what was his.

LONE GUN
Eric Allen

Smoke Blackbird had been away too long. The Lequires had seized the Blackbird farm, forcing the Indians and settlers off, and no one seemed willing to fight! He had to fight alone.

THE THIRD RIDER
Barry Cord

Mel Rawlins wasn't going to let anything stand in his way. His father was murdered, his two brothers gone. Now Mel rode for vengeance.